He's determined to set things right, no matter the cost.

The last person Abby Crawford wants to face down is country music superstar Seth Kendall. Last time she did, she flat-out lied so he'd go to Nashville without her. She's never understood why their mutual best friend proposed, but she went with it so her baby wouldn't be fatherless. Now she's a divorced mother of a teenager, and secretly Seth's biggest fan.

Seth is home in McAllister, Texas for his father's funeral…and a chance to meet the daughter he's never known. He's willing to face the music of his own making and admit he's known about his little girl all along. For fifteen years he's kept his distance because Abby told him to follow his dreams without her, insisting she didn't love him. But now he won't leave until he knows his daughter and she knows him, even if it means facing the woman who broke his heart for good.

Confessing she's lied about her daughter's paternity all these years won't be easy for Abby, especially with her ex blackmailing her to keep the secret. And Seth doesn't know the hardest truth of all: Every love song he plays on his guitar still plucks her heartstrings.

Books by Sara Walter Ellwood

Colton Gambers Series
Gambling On A Secret, Book One
Gambling On A Heart, Book Two
Gambling On A Dream, Book Three

Heartstrings

Published by Kensington Publishing Corporation

Heartstrings

Sara Walter Ellwood

LYRICAL PRESS
Kensington Publishing Corp.
www.kensingtonbooks.com

First Electronic Edition: April 2013
eISBN-13: 978-1-61650-455-7
eISBN-10: 1-61650-455-2

First Print Edition: April 2013
ISBN-13: 978-1-61650-868-5
ISBN-10: 1-61650-868-X

Printed in the United States of America

To the musicians in my family...

Marcus and Laura.

I love you!

Acknowledgements

First, I have to thank my amazing critique partners, D'Ann Lindun, Chloe Blaire, and Martha Ramirez for all the times they read and reread this story through its various incarnations. I will forever be indebted to these wonderful writers for all their hard work and valuable time.
Secondly, I have to thank my editor, Piper Denna. She is awesome, and I'm so glad fate brought us together.
And never lastly, I have to thank my family for their love and continued support. I love you.

Foreword

I've always been a fan of country music. When I was little, I'd dress up in my prettiest dress and my grandma's sofa doilies and stand on her coffee table, belting out at the top of my lungs to her old 8-tracks of Dolly Parton and Kenny Rogers. For years, I had the words to Dolly's Jolene and Kenny's The Gambler memorized and could sing them at a drop of a hat.

My big dream of being the next Dolly Parton was quickly squashed when my third grade music teacher told me I couldn't hold a tune in a bucket and refused to let me in the school chorus. Granted, I still can't sing, but I often find myself humming those old country songs.

Heartstrings is my tribute to my love of country music. It is also a study of determination. This story has been through more rewrites than I can count. But in the end, I think it's one of my favorites. I hope you fall as much in love with Seth, Abby and Emily as I have.

Thank you, from the bottom of my heart.

Love,
Sara

Prologue

December 1983

Seth tightened his arms around his father's neck and stared down at Momma lying on the bed of white in the big box. Daddy had cried last night. He'd never seen his daddy cry before. Not even last summer when Ol' Blue died. The coonhound had been his hunting dog forever. Something bad must be wrong.

"Daddy, why won't Momma wake up?"

His father rubbed his back and held him closer. He trembled as he spoke. "Your momma went away, buddy. She can't come home."

He pulled away. "Like Ol' Blue did?"

Daddy swallowed so hard his throat moved up and down. "Yeah, son. Just like Ol' Blue."

He looked back at Momma. She was so pretty. Her yellow hair fixed in a fancy hairdo, and her face all made up as if she were going out to sing somewhere.

Daddy hated Momma's singing. They fought about it all the time. "Daddy, I heard you and Momma fighting the other night." He turned back to meet his father's eyes again. "What's a divorce? And why did you call Momma a--a *whore*?"

Daddy glanced around as several of the other people standing nearby looked at them. He carried him over to a chair against the wall and sat with him on his lap. "You don't need to worry about that."

Momma never was like Mike's mom. Carolann played with Mike and his baby sister and even Seth, and Abby when her mom brought her over to play. Carolann baked cookies and made up games.

Momma never had time for him or his friends. She always seemed so sad. The only time she was happy was when she was getting ready to go out. Momma drank a lot of grown-up drinks and acted mad all the time.

When she'd take some of those little pills she hid in her dresser drawer in her room, she'd be happy, but she still never had time for him.

"Momma said she hated us."

The next morning after she'd said that, Momma wouldn't wake up. The sheriff had come and asked Daddy a bunch of questions.

Daddy held him close and kissed the top of his head. "Your momma loved you, Seth. She just…just…" His voice cracked and he sounded like he was crying again. "She just never forgave me for not letting her go off to Nashville."

"Why?"

"I was afraid she'd get famous and forget about us." Daddy pulled him close, his voice so low and deep he had to listen close to hear the words. "Instead, she felt trapped here and hated me for denying her dream."

If Momma hated Daddy, she probably hated him, too.

Chapter 1

Seth Kendall parked his Escalade and stared out at the people who had known him all his life. What the hell was he doing here?

With a sigh, he opened the door, and all eyes turned in his direction as he got out. Why hadn't he stayed in Nashville as everyone assumed he would? Why did coming back here seem so important now, after being away for fourteen years?

The answers to those questions had plagued him the entire drive to his hometown of McAllister in the Texas Panhandle. The motivation wasn't his father's death at all. He'd come home because it was time for him to make things right, even if that meant causing a whole mess of hell to get it done.

He shrugged into his jacket. If it had been made of solid iron, it wouldn't have felt any heavier. The mid-August day was hot, but the sweat gathering under his Hugo Boss suit didn't come from the afternoon sun. People watched him all the time. That came with the fame he'd garnered as a country music superstar, but today, he didn't want to be gawked at. He adjusted the knot of his necktie and closed the door of the SUV.

He tipped his hat and nodded toward his father's friends and business associates as he headed toward the old church. None of the mourners spoke to him, but he could imagine what they were thinking. Everyone knew he and his father had despised each other.

Decorum required he remove his Ray-Bans and black Stetson as he entered the church, but he forced his expression to remain impassive. He combed his fingers through his hair and looked around. People chose seats, gradually filling the oak pews, and the low murmur of conversation mingled with the bagpipes playing a mournful rendition of his father's favorite hymn, *Amazing Grace*. He recognized almost everyone as he made his way to the front.

"Aunt Johanna." He stopped where his father's twin sister and the minister were speaking in hushed tones next to the open casket.

Johanna Kendall looked up at him with blue eyes reminding him of his father's. Dressed in a severe black dress and with her graying red hair pulled into a bun, she stepped forward and wrapped him in a hug. "Seth, I'm glad you finally made it home."

He held on for a moment before letting go. He'd come home for her. "How are you holding up?"

She shrugged and her eyes filled with misty sadness. "I'll be okay." Johanna used a white lace handkerchief to dab at her red-rimmed eyes. "I'll miss him. I never realized his heart was so bad. He always seemed as strong as a bull."

"We may not have seen eye to eye, but he was still my father." Hugging his aunt again, he held her and looked anywhere but at the man lying on the white satin inside the casket. He glanced at the pew behind him. As he sucked in a deep breath, he stepped away from Johanna and dropped his hat onto the seat.

Johanna moved away to speak with Glenda Marshall, the mayor's wife.

Seth held out his hand to the minister. "Reverend Keller."

"It's a shame you were unable to get away from your engagements to come home sooner. How're you doin', Seth?"

"I'm as good as can be expected, I guess." He shook the preacher's hand, then shoved both of his hands into his pants pockets. "I'm glad he didn't suffer." He didn't know what else to say.

He'd been in the recording studio when Johanna had frantically called him three days ago after she'd found John dead on the floor of his study. Unsure if he'd come home for the funeral or not, he finished the last songs for his next album, set for release in the spring. Now he wished he hadn't rushed to get the damned record done. At least then, he'd have had an excuse to escape as soon as this day was over.

Which was complete bullshit. He wasn't leaving here until he settled a score.

A heavy hand touched his shoulder. He turned to look into the rich brown eyes of one of his father's closest friends, and a man for whom he held a great deal of respect. He stuck out his hand and greeted the older man with a warm smile. "Judge Ritter, it's great to see you again."

Retired county judge Franklin Michael Ritter II smiled and shook his hand. He'd always reminded Seth a little of Mark Twain--tall and lanky with white wavy hair and a handlebar mustache. "It's nice to see you, too.

Though, I'd have preferred different circumstances. It's been a long time, son."

He didn't miss the quiet censure in the judge's tone. Or the way the man seemed to shake all over. His Parkinson's must have gotten worse.

"Oh, Seth, I'm so glad you made it home," an extremely petite woman said in a soft Georgia accent, and Seth found himself being hugged tightly around the waist. He returned Carolann Ritter's embrace, holding on for a moment. In so many ways, she'd replaced the mother he'd lost to a drug overdose. "We sorely did miss you over the years."

He forced a smile as she stepped away. Guilt needled him when tears shimmered in her brown eyes. Carolann and Frank had never made it a secret they loved him when he was a kid. Lord knew he never heard those words from his old man.

"Aw, Miz Ritter, I've missed y'all, too."

When a woman slowly moved in next to Carolann and Frank Ritter, his heart constricted. He forced the name through his tightening jaw. "Abigail."

"Hello, Seth." Dressed in a simple navy blue dress, Abigail Crawford Ritter stopped before him. She stared up at him with widened almond-shaped eyes the color of brandy. The naturally tan complexion she'd inherited from her Native American mother went pale and taut over her high cheekbones. She fiddled with the purse strap over her shoulder and pulled her long dark brown hair over her other shoulder. "We didn't think you'd be here."

He easily discerned the real meaning: *We don't want you here.*

The past slammed into him with blazing force, transporting him back to the manmade beach of the McAllister Reservoir. Returning him to the night he and Abby let their attraction turn into uncontrolled lust, and under the stars on a deserted stretch of weedy sand, she'd given him her virginity.

"Uh...I wasn't sure...I would be," he stammered and tried to shake off the memory of a passion he hadn't been able to forget. He forced himself to look beyond her.

"Sorry about your father." Mike Ritter stepped forward. His brown eyes were as hard as the bricks making up the walls of the church. Not quite reaching six feet, Mike was four inches shorter, and lanky like Frank. Mike was dressed in a suit as expensive as Seth's, if not more so. Since when was the county paying its sheriff enough for him to afford an Armani suit and snakeskin boots? Not to mention the Resistol hat in his hand.

Then Seth noticed the obviously pregnant brunette holding Mike's hand. An heiress to a fortune made from the railroad, oil and banking. "Tammy Jo McAllister?"

She smiled and slipped her arm around Mike's waist, while she rested her other hand on her baby bump. The gray dress she wore had *designer* written all over it. She must still have more money than King Midas and spent it like there was no tomorrow. "Hello, Seth. I'm now Tammy Jo Ritter."

An icy weight settled in his gut as he looked at Abby. She averted her eyes to the floor. "Mike and I were divorced two years ago."

The weight grew larger and radiated into his arms and legs. He couldn't keep coldness from leaking into his words. "Well, isn't that interesting? How's Emily?"

Abby's face lost all color as she looked at Frank and Carolann. Damn, they'd never learned the truth.

Mike's voice held an unmistakable warning not to push the issue. "Thanks for asking. She's fine."

He met Mike's glare with one of his own.

"I think we should sit down," she said in shaky voice before he could respond.

He snapped his gaze to Abby. Her eyes blazed with anger. She clenched her hands so tightly her knuckles bleached white against the dark blue of her skirt.

"I didn't realize you knew our granddaughter," Frank said without the least bit of curiosity. He obviously didn't catch any of the byplay.

I should know her. He'd keep up Abby's charade. For now.

"He met her at a concert in Amarillo." Mike's tone left no room for discussion on the blatant lie. "I think we should catch up on old times. After the service."

Seth glanced away from the cold eyes of the man who'd been his best friend growing up. Abby's dark eyes held no welcome either, which was a sucker punch in the gut. He wanted to see fire in Abby's brown eyes, but not from hatred.

"Yeah." He mentally shook himself. What was he thinking? She'd betrayed him. He looked back at Mike. "I think it's time to talk about those old times."

* * * *

Abby had feared this encounter since the moment her mother-in-law had called her with the news of John Kendall's death. She took her seat behind the Ritters and fisted her hands in her lap.

Mike had promised this day would never come, but she knew it would. How could she have been so stupid? She opened her hands, and cooling air hit the fine sheen of moisture coating her palms. Cold perspiration beaded on her forehead, and she resisted the urge to wipe it away. She had to control her emotions. If she wasn't careful, someone would notice her anxiety.

Mike glanced over his shoulder at her. He'd always been the solid one, her rock. He grounded her while Seth had been her dream. Her flight of fantasy. The one thing she could never really hold. Even now, even after their sham of a marriage had long ago dissolved into nothing but friendship, she had faith Mike would make everything all right.

Mike had stood by her when Seth left town to chase his dreams in Nashville. Seth had promised her he'd come home, he'd always be here for her, but he hadn't stuck around. He'd left and never came back.

Tammy Jo leaned against Mike's shoulder, and he shifted his focus to his new wife, wrapping his arm around her shoulders.

As Revered Keller began speaking about the kind of man her neighbor had been in life, she sensed Seth's attention on her and couldn't concentrate on anything the pastor said regarding John Kendall. Halfway through the service, she dared to look across the aisle at Seth. His gaze seemed to bore into hers, and the bitterness in the green depths of his eyes seared deep into her soul.

There had been a time when she was his second-best friend. She knew his secrets, and he knew hers, even things Mike hadn't known about them. She'd believed in Seth's dreams, had encouraged them when his father degraded and beat him for having them. In return, Seth had always been there for her when she'd needed someone to take her away from the reality of her life of living down her parents' sins.

She'd fallen in love with Seth, but she knew they had no future. Maybe if he hadn't wanted fame and fortune, they could have found a way to a happily-ever-after. Keeping him here would have destroyed him. And if she'd gone with him, it would have ruined them both. When Seth won a place on the new talent show *America's Rising Star*, she'd had to let him go--even if it meant lying to him to make him leave. But the passion they'd shared had haunted her ever since.

At the service's end, she met Seth's gaze across the aisle again. He had no intention of letting her forget what happened after that night on the beach when everything changed.

* * * *

The service had been typical and, thankfully, neither Johanna nor anyone else seemed to expect Seth to stand and give a eulogy, or worse, sing. He followed the hearse outside town to the Kendall family plot in a small grove of live oaks on the Double K Ranch where five generations of Kendalls were buried.

He had to talk to Abby. He wasn't the same boy who'd left her standing on her front porch the night he'd left town. But one thing hadn't changed; he'd never forgiven her for what she'd done after that night.

He got out of his SUV, went around, and opened the passenger door for Johanna. She leaned on him to help her out of the high vehicle, then they moved to stand beside the grave.

The scene of the pallbearers unloading his father's casket from the back of the hearse overshadowed his need to confront Abby. The oppressive midday sun beat down on him and glistened off the gray granite of the tombstone marking the grave where his father would be laid to rest. His gaze fell on the name of the woman he barely remembered.

Suzann Harris Kendall, born May 14, 1960, died July 28, 1983. May her voice charm the angels of heaven.

His mother. Dead at age twenty-three. He recalled that day almost thirty years ago when he'd stood here with his father and family. That day he'd wondered if his mother would hate him from heaven for ruining her life by simply being born.

It was a question he still wondered about.

A heavy lump settled in the pit of his stomach.

Dad, will you hate me in death for doing what you denied of my mother? For having dreams that didn't include you and making them come true?

He and his father hadn't had a relationship since he was about ten years old, when John had beat him for sneaking into the barn to play his mother's old guitar. But before then, his dad had been everything to him.

The first wave of regret hit him hard as memories of his early childhood fluttered to the surface, such as the Christmas when he was five and his father had given him his first fishing rod.

"You'll be sure to catch some big ones with that, son."

"Can we go now?"

"Not yet." His father ruffled his hair and grinned. *"But as soon as spring comes, we'll go to the lake, and I'll teach you how to fly fish."*

"Can Mike come along?"

John chuckled. "You bet. I think Santa Claus brought him the same thing. And if you'd like, we can bring Abby, too." He winked and added, "I'm sure we can find a fishin' rod she can use."

"Yahoo!"

Like the photographs in an album, the snippets of his childhood passed over his mind's eye. So many things from happier times.

"It's my one chance, Dad. Why are you doing this? Ruining my mother's dreams wasn't enough, now you have to ruin mine, too? I'm going to Nashville. I'm going to sing in that competition and I'll win. I'll get that record deal."

"If you leave, don't bother comin' back. You won't be welcome."

The bitterness of hateful words yelled in a fit of rage settled upon him. His back hurt with a phantom sting from all the times the belt had hit him. The shotgun his father fired the time he returned after winning the talent competition blasted his ears. The memory album slammed shut, smothering the spark of grief.

He swallowed the anger and the urge to drive away and never look back.

He looked up to see Abby watching him. No, he wasn't going anywhere.

At least, not until he claimed what his fear of becoming like his mother--washed-up and dead by age twenty-three--had denied him. The one person he'd let Mike talk him out of ever getting to know, by playing on his fears.

His daughter.

* * * *

The old Victorian house on the Double K Ranch was packed with mourners from the funeral. The Ladies' Auxiliary served beef barbeque sandwiches, baked beans, potato salad, and chocolate cake.

Abby had no appetite, but she carried her loaded plate out of the dining room with its old over-sized furniture to the wide wraparound porch. Several people milled around in small clusters, holding their plates and doing more talking than eating.

She smiled and greeted those who talked to her--not that many people did, but she didn't stop--and continued searching for Seth. She had to find out what he intended to do now that he was back in McAllister.

"Do you think Seth will stay in town?"

She stopped and took a deep breath before facing the woman behind her. Tammy Jo had never liked her, but then she'd never quite understood what Mike had ever seen in the spoiled heiress.

"I doubt it. He's famous. Nothing in McAllister mattered to him before." She turned to move away from her ex-husband's wife.

"I overheard him talking with his aunt."

When Abby looked at her, Tammy Jo smiled and glanced around at the people on the porch. She could barely keep the disdain off her supermodel face. So, she still considered herself better than the rest of them.

Tammy Jo met her gaze again and her smile widened. "Seth asked her what his father planned for the ranch. Seems to me he's thinking of moving here. How wonderful that would be. He's so famous."

"Yeah, wonderful," she muttered. Of course, Tammy Jo would think so, now that Seth Kendall was famous and rich. But there had been a time she wouldn't have given Seth a second glance.

Abby looked around again. She hadn't seen Seth since arriving at the house after leaving the gravesite.

She'd see about him staying. He had no business here. He'd promised to come back. Oh, he'd come back all right, only to leave again. He hadn't even wanted to see his baby. Chasing his dreams had been more important. Now, he could just keep on chasing them.

The numbed part of her heart belonging to Seth Kendall started to beat. The hurt was unbearable at the thought he'd leave her again.

Which was totally ridiculous. He had to go. His showing up now in Emily's life would serve no purpose but to devastate her.

Mike walked up beside her and Tammy Jo. He smiled at his wife and kissed her on the cheek. She rested her hand on her seven-month baby bump and looked up at him with softness in her hazel eyes.

Mike glanced at Abby and then back to Tammy Jo. Abby's heart skipped a beat at the answering love he held for his wife in his eyes. He'd never looked upon her like that, but then, neither she nor Mike had ever been in love.

"Sweetheart, I need to talk to Abby about Emily. Can you go find Miz Kendall and make sure she's doing okay? She's taking John's death hard."

Tammy Jo's smile turned cold. "Of course." High heels clicked across the porch as she strode into the kitchen.

The screen door closed with a bang, making Abby cringe. "You know she hates me."

Mike swallowed and looked down at his hands. "She thinks you have some hold over me." He met her gaze before turning away and heading off the porch. "C'mon."

She set her plate of untouched food on the wide banister and followed Mike out onto the lawn. They passed Martha Gordon and two of Tammy

Jo's elderly aunts she took care of, as they sat under the trees in the garden eating and chatting. Mike nodded and tipped his hat at the older women.

"Sheriff Ritter, how you doin'? Getting ready for that baby?" Martha's smile showed extra bright against her dark brown complexion.

"I'm doing fine, Miz Gordon. And I can't wait until Tammy Jo has the baby." He smiled as they continued walking. "Aunts Edna and Bea. Good to see you ladies out and about."

The spinster sisters harrumphed and glared at Abby.

Martha glanced at the sisters and then back to her. "Good to see you, dear. The nursing home keepin' you busy these days?"

She didn't miss the curiosity in the woman's words, or the McAllister sisters' lips compressed into stern lines. "You too, Mrs. Gordon. Yes, I'm picking up some of Darlene Martinez's hours."

"Glad to hear you ain't causin' trouble."

Mike raised a brow at her and then looked over his shoulder at the women. "We leave all the trouble to our daughter."

Martha chuckled. "Now, I just bet that sweet little girl can cause a heap of trouble. But she sure was blessed with an angel's voice. Will she be singing at the Founder's Day picnic next month?"

Abby glanced at Mike before answering. Neither of them wanted Emily to sing publicly, but they also had long realized she had too much of her father in her to keep her quiet. "You know she will."

Edna leaned closer to her sister and said just loud enough for Abby to hear, "I remember John having the same trouble with Seth. That boy would sing to the cows just to spite his daddy. God rest his soul."

Abby's breath caught at the comparison.

Mike held her gaze a beat before tipping his hat and smiling at the women again. "Have a good afternoon, ladies."

Once they rounded the corner of the house and were out of earshot of the elderly women, Abby said, "Do you think people wonder where Emily's talent comes from?"

"No." He set his hand on her back and guided her to the white rail fence bordering the yard. "Talent may run in families, but that doesn't automatically mean it has to. Besides, I have a cousin from Georgia who is a rock singer. So, talent does run in my family if anyone ever asks."

He'd eased her mind a little. "You're probably right." She smiled and glanced at Mike as he looked out over the pastures. "You know most people think I'm hanging around you and your family because I want you back."

Sara Walter Ellwood

Mike met her gaze and shoved his hands into his pockets. "We were pretty convincing when we were married. Our divorce surprised the whole town."

"Yeah, we deserve an Academy Award for that performance."

"What's that supposed to mean?"

She laughed and waved the comment off. "Nothing. It's just amazing how easily we fooled everyone." She leaned over the fence rail and stared at the cattle grazing on the buffalo grass. "Thank you. I don't know what I would've done without you." She met his deep brown eyes and smiled. "And I'm also sorry."

"For what?"

She straightened and faced him as she pushed her hair from her face. A warm breeze blew across the flat grassland of the pastures. "You know what for. You and Tammy Jo. You were so head over heels crazy for her in high school. I wish I'd have known about your affair sooner. I'd have let you go then. It's the least I could have done."

She'd be lying to herself if she said his secret two-year affair with Tammy Jo hadn't hurt, but she couldn't be what Mike needed. She loved him, but not as a woman should love her husband. He'd always been more like a big brother to her. Her best friend.

Seth had been the one she'd burned for during those long nights while Mike slept on the far side of their bed. He never felt passion for her either. Soon after their marriage, they stopped trying to find it. Their nearly non-existent sex life had always been damned awkward.

He looked away and leaned his backside against a fence post. "I've always loved her. But I couldn't turn my back on you--or Emily."

He squinted against the glare of the sun. She'd always known what Mike sacrificed to be with her, to be a father to her baby, giving them a stable home.

The one thing she never understood was why he'd made the sacrifice. But now wasn't the time to ask. Of course, he wouldn't have told her anyway. He never had any of the other times she'd asked.

"Tammy Jo seems to be taking pregnancy well."

Mike chuckled and seemed to peer down at his expensive rattlesnake boots. He'd left his suit jacket in his Mercedes, and the tie must be there, too. Tammy Jo might be able to dress Mike up to look the part as a member the upper crust of society, but deep down Mike Ritter was still a cowboy who'd never wanted to do anything but ride rodeo.

"She is," he said. "The decorator just finished the baby's room. You ought to see it. The suite is fit for a prince."

She could imagine the expense of remodeling the old mansion in the center of town would probably feed a small country for a year too.

"So, she's having a boy?"

When he turned to her, the purest joy shone in his dark, warm eyes. "Yeah. But you have to swear to secrecy. Tammy Jo wants it to be a surprise for everyone."

She pushed loose hair from her face again, twisted the long mane and pulled it over her shoulder. "You got it. I'm happy for you. You always wanted a son."

The warm breeze ruffled the blond hair on his forehead under his hat brim. "That doesn't change what I feel for Emily. You know that, right?" He focused on her again. "I love her, Abby. That will never change. I've loved her since that first time I felt her kick when you were about four months pregnant. You remember that?"

"Yeah. You thought she was surely part bronco."

The large yard stretched in front of her. She, Mike and Seth had played a lot of tag and hide-and-seek on this patch of grass. A storm must be brewing somewhere. She folded her arms against the sudden chill in the air and hoped it didn't come to destroy their lives.

"You are her father in every way that matters. I know you love her." Facing him, she leaned her shoulder against a fencepost. "Mike, what are we going to do? Tammy Jo said she overheard Seth voicing an interest in the ranch. If he inherits the Double K and stays, what will we tell your parents? They adore Emily. But I'm not sure I can keep Emily in the dark if he's here. She idolizes him."

He took her by the hand and squeezed. His eyes flashed with anger. "We don't tell them a damned thing," he said, his voice pitched low. "Especially Emily. Besides, what claim does he have on her? My name's on her birth certificate. You said so yourself--I'm her father. He left you. He abandoned Emily. Hell, he came to the house and practically gloated, since I was married to you, he was relieved he didn't have to be saddled with a baby." He brushed his fingers over her cheek. "Abby, we can't tell anyone. Do you understand what the truth would do to them? To Emily?

She nodded and clutched the folds of her skirt. The falsehood suddenly rubbed wrong on the painful spot in her heart belonging to Seth. "I suppose."

He smiled and stepped away from the railing. "I better get back before someone sees us and thinks the unthinkable." He squeezed her hand again before letting it go. "Abby, I've always been your friend. Nothing's changed. I'm here if you need me. Don't let your feelings for Seth sway you. Keeping Emily away from him is best for her. Think about how finding out about this will affect Mom. None of us want to bury her next."

She nodded and smiled, but it felt forced. He was right. Carolann's sick heart couldn't take the pain or the stress if she discovered the truth about her only grandchild. "I know. Now, get back in there to that jealous wife of yours."

He ambled across the yard and went around the corner of the house. She hugged herself and made her way to the old gazebo in the corner of the green expanse of grass. A grove of pecan trees provided shade for the structure. She plunged into the cool darkness when she stepped under the deeply pitched roof. Her eyes took a moment to adjust to the dimness.

She ran her hand over the chipped white paint of the banister.

"Remember when you, Mike and I painted this old thing?"

At the sound of the deep voice, she spun, her hand going over her heart. Seth stood up from the swing hanging from the rafters on the other side. "Seth..."

She sucked in a breath and it caught in her throat. Time had changed him, but it had also made him even more devastatingly handsome. The dark tailored pants showed off his long legs and above-average height. The white dress shirt fit like a custom glove, outlining his broad shoulders. He'd lost the power tie he'd worn to the funeral. The top two buttons of his shirt lay open, and he'd rolled the sleeves to his elbows, showing off powerful forearms.

His coppery-blond hair curled over his collar and fell over his high forehead. A trimmed ginger-colored goatee hid the scar on his chin from a riding accident. The green ice of his eyes captured her gaze and made her heart race.

He gestured toward the pasture with a tall glass of what looked and smelled like whiskey. "I saw you and Mike. So, what happened? I thought you two would be together forever."

She shrugged and turned away from him as he took a long sip from the glass. "I don't see how that's any of your damned business."

A board in the floor creaked as he approached. She looked over her shoulder. He was so close. Her heart stuttered over a beat or two and something warm curled in her belly. How could he still affect her after everything he'd done to her?

He smiled, but it never reached his eyes. They remained two stormy seas ready to devour her in their relentless waves. "Oh, but I think it is very much my business. I want to see my daughter, Abigail."

"You lost that right when you drove away that night." She fisted her hands and faced him. "You lost that right when you let another man take your place in her life."

He narrowed his eyes and leaned closer. His breath reeked from the whiskey. She wrinkled her nose at the painful memories of her father's addiction to alcohol as much as from the stench.

"You know why I had to leave. It was my one and only chance. Goddamn it, you didn't give me any other option."

She snorted and squared her shoulders. "You had fame and fortune to chase. I'm glad you achieved your dreams. But it came with a price."

"I told you I'd be back. But when I returned you were married to my best friend."

"You were gone for seven months!" She gritted her teeth against the old hurt. "You never called or wrote, but I watched that damned talent show every week and cheered you on. Then the next thing I heard, you were dating Amanda Lang from the show. I figured you made your choice. You wanted no part of me or my baby. So, I made mine."

"Amanda and I were and are just friends. The media blew that whole duet thing out of proportion. It wasn't until I found out you were married and gave away my little girl that we became friends with benefits."

The memory of watching them together on the show churned inside her. Maybe the media had taken an innocent friendship of two teenagers and attached a connotation that wasn't there. Still, he couldn't deny he and the blond, green-eyed pop star started dating two weeks after he returned to Nashville after his winning the show and had been in an on again-off again relationship for years.

He looked into his glass of whiskey. "I'm sorry I didn't call or write. I was eighteen and scared shitless. I had to concentrate on winning, but the whole time I was thinking about you."

She laughed, but instead of coming out bitter, it scratched and resounded with too much raw pain. "You were scared? What the hell do you think I was? I was seventeen and pregnant. My father was dying with a brain tumor, and I had a ranch to run."

He grabbed her arm when she spun away. "I had to sing in that competition. Otherwise, it would've taken ten years to get to the kind of success I got from winning *America's Rising Star*. If I ever got that chance again. My mother never did. This place killed her. I couldn't let that happen to me. Or to you and our baby."

She swallowed but couldn't work her constricted throat.

"I wanted you to come with me." His voice dipped low enough it might have been on the verge of cracking. "I wanted you and our baby, Abigail. You are the one who turned your back on me. You're the one who couldn't wait to fall into bed with my best friend."

Oh, how she wished she could tell him the truth about her and Mike, but she wouldn't. She glared at his hand on her upper arm, then at him. "You're drunk. Let go, now."

He stepped back, letting go. She was amazed at how calm she'd sounded, because inside her a twister had taken up residence. Her heart raced and her jaw and hands ached from clenching tightly. "You knew why I couldn't run off to Nashville with you and live on dreams and fairytales. Mike understood, and he was here when I needed him. He gave me what you wouldn't."

But neither of them knew the real reason she didn't go with Seth.

When she reached the grass again, she turned toward him and folded her arms in front of her. "If you're thinking about staying here, you can forget it. I don't want you around. My being divorced has nothing to do with you. Mike is still Emily's father, and that's how it's going to stay."

She blinked against the burn in her eyes. Damn, if she didn't soon get out of here, she'd start bawling. "Go back to your fast cars and even faster women. Go back to your stadiums full of groupies and your high life as a Grammy-winning superstar. McAllister, Texas, has nothing for you. It never has."

Chapter 2

Seth walked up the stone pathway to the front of the Spanish style house of the Circle R Ranch. He had a lot of fond memories of the old place. Carolann always had a way of making him feel welcome and wanted.

Dear God, how he'd wished his mother could have been more like her when he was little. Then after his father had changed and become mean and started hitting him, he wished he could have moved in with the Ritters. That he and Mike were real brothers and he wouldn't have to go home ever again.

He looked past the barn. New white paint reflected the late afternoon sun. Black Angus cattle fed on the grass and sleek horses stood in the corral. During his and Mike's senior year, the cattle had been sold off to pay the mounting debts, and the only horses around had been two old swayback mares.

Frank had served his first term as county judge then, but he had never been a good manager of finances. He'd run the place to the ground and was living from hand to mouth for years.

He looked back at the house. It, too, had been updated with amenities it hadn't had fifteen years ago. The pool was new, as was the four-car garage in front of which was parked a fancy black sports car. He recognized the Mercedes from the funeral. Mike and Tammy Jo.

He took another deep breath and headed up the steps to the front door. He might have an ulterior motive for showing up at Thursday supper, but Carolann had invited him, and he wanted to visit with her and Frank. If he met his daughter while here, so be it.

The thought scared the hell out of him.

What would she think of him? Could she ever understand why he had to leave? His father had demanded he give up singing after high school. He couldn't give it up any more than he could breathing. The talent show had been his only real chance to get out of Texas and make his dreams come true.

He'd come back, but it was too late. Abby had already given his baby away. She'd already given her heart to someone else. He'd wanted to see his little girl over the years, but every time he'd gathered his courage to come home, Mike's words burned in his mind.

What kind of father do you think you'll be, Seth?

With the reminder of his parents' messed up lives, he'd convinced himself Emily was better off never knowing him.

Until now.

He tucked the bottle of red wine he'd brought under his arm and gripped the handle of his guitar case tighter with a sweaty hand. According to Frank, Emily was quite a fan of his.

Something sweet and warm curled inside his heart.

When the door opened after he rang the doorbell, he expected Carolann. Instead, he met the wide green eyes of a tall, thin, auburn-haired girl who resembled a combination of Abby and his Granny Kendall too much to be a fluke.

Jesus, she was beautiful.

He rubbed his goatee and forced air through his constricting voice box to form words. "You must be...Emily?" He swallowed the lump in his throat and painted on a smile. "I'm guessing you already know who I am."

But she didn't know him at all. Dear God, he was this girl's father.

She swung the door open, and the shock turned into the biggest and brightest smile he'd ever seen. The force of it hit his solar plexus like a fist.

She held out her hand. "I'm Emily Ritter. Hi."

He looked at her hand, and a million different feelings tumbled through him--fear, joy, amazement, excitement and so many more, he couldn't keep track. He doubted a blind man seeing a sunrise for the first time could feel this happy. Trembling, he encircled her warm fingers with his big hand.

You're my little girl.

The baby he'd tried for fifteen years to forget about and never quite succeeded.

Her grip was soft and cool and her fingers trembled. Good, maybe she didn't feel just how badly his shook.

When he let go, she balled her hand into a loose fist, held it over her heart and giggled. "I'd have to be blind, deaf and dumb not to know who you are. But that wouldn't be an excuse in my family. Please come in, Mr. Kendall."

Inside the foyer, he set his guitar case next to the wall and hung his hat on the hat rack by the door. Only one other hat hung on the hooks. He stared at Mike's thousand-dollar tan Resistol, and rage boiled the bile in his belly.

He yanked his gaze from the hat and smiled at his baby. "Please call me Seth."

She blushed and nodded. "Okay, Seth it is. Grandma's in the kitchen. Everyone else is out back on the patio."

He followed her down the hall to the big open kitchen. Carolann turned away from the counter where she was tossing a salad. She smiled and wiped her hands on her white apron.

"I brought red wine." He set the bottle on the island counter. "I think it's still chilled."

"Thank you. Emily, why don't you set it in the fridge for now." She walked around the island and hugged him. He towered over her petite, five-foot frame. "I'm so glad you could make it." When she stepped away, she glanced at Emily, who closed the refrigerator door and shoved her hands into the back pockets of her denim shorts. "I told you I had a surprise for you."

Emily averted her eyes and sucked her bottom lip between her teeth. Abby used to do the same thing when she was embarrassed.

"Emily idolizes you." Carolann smiled up at him again. "She prances around singing your songs all the time."

"Grandma!" Emily's eyes widened.

Carolann raised a brow. "Did I tell a lie?" She winked at him. "Of course, that isn't as embarrassing as some of the stories I could tell about him."

He laughed on cue, but it was strangled and forced.

Emily shook her head. "I have all of your music downloaded on my iPod. I can sing and play piano and guitar. And I talked Mom and Dad into letting me sing at the Founder's Day picnic next month." She blushed as red as her tank top and looked down at the floor. "I hope you don't mind. I'd like to sing some of your songs."

His heart beat so fast and hard he feared it was going to pound right out of his chest. He couldn't concentrate on anything except that he and Abby had created this--this person, together.

"Seth, are you all right?" Carolann's warm touch on his arm and the concern lacing her soft southern voice drove a hole through the fog surrounding him.

He blinked. "I'm sorry. I guess I'm just a little...I just...just thought of Dad..." he lied. He shook his head, trying to clear it.

Emily wanted to sing his songs? Dear God, his chest hurt. He put his hand over his heart.

Carolann patted his arm. "I understand perfectly. It's never easy losing someone. Even someone you didn't think you cared a fig about."

He nodded agreement, but it wasn't losing his father that had him turned upside down and inside out.

The kitchen door opened. "Mom, how much longer? Dad's getting antsy..." Mike's words died on his lips when he walked into the kitchen. His gaze hardened and snapped to Emily.

Carolann picked up the large salad bowl, and a wide smile lit up her face. "Michael, be a dear and take this out to the patio and tell your father dinner will be ready in a few minutes."

Mike made no move to take the bowl. "Emily, do as your grandmother asked. I'd like to have a minute with Seth."

Emily's face fell and she huffed. "But, Daddy..."

Mike raised a brow, and she reached for the bowl with all the drama only a fourteen-year-old girl could muster.

Carolann looked from Mike to Emily as she handed the bowl to her. "Don't worry. You'll have plenty of time to bend Seth's ears."

Mike waited until Emily exited through the kitchen door and Carolann headed for the pantry before moving toward the hall to the living room. Seth followed him into the front room.

Mike slid the pocket door closed before turning loose the fury in his saddle-brown eyes. "What the hell are you doing, showing up here?"

Seth turned away and walked around the familiar room slowly. He, Mike and Abby had done their share of romping in here. "I'm here for dinner. Your parents invited me."

Mike watched him with his hands fisted by his sides and his feet apart. "You should have declined."

"And disappoint your momma? I don't think so." He stopped at the mantle with its display of family photos. He picked one up of Mike holding baby Emily. He was all smiles and looked every bit the proud papa.

Something in him broke. A floodgate that held back more than a decade of pain and betrayal. He returned the frame with a shaky hand.

This time, the trembling wasn't from overwhelming amazement, but barely controlled anger.

He turned and worked to keep his temper in check. "I only have one question for you." He had to unclench his back teeth to chew out the words. "Why did you marry Abby?"

Mike moved the lace curtain to look out the front window. "I loved her." His voice was low and as cold as a Montana wind in mid-January. "That's more than can be said for you. You only wanted a piece of ass." Dropping the lace, Mike turned and faced him with a sneer twisting his pretty-boy face. His eyes were as icy as his voice. "I told you that when we had this very same discussion after Emily was born, if I recall."

Seth took a step closer and grabbed his shirt. Mike's voice from that day fourteen years ago echoed in his mind.

"What kind of father do you think you'll be, Seth? Yours is a son-of-a-bitch to you most of the time. Your mother killed herself just because she had to live the simple life like the rest of us. Abby and I are married. You'll be away more than you'll ever be here. I'm not going anywhere. I love that baby, Seth. I love her. What do you feel for her?"

At the time, he hadn't known what he felt. How wrong had he been? About Mike being a better father than he could ever be. And about not fighting for his right to be a father to the little girl who'd stolen his heart without him ever seeing her. "You didn't give me a chance to be her father. You didn't even allow me to see her."

Mike pushed his hand away and stepped back. "I'm not fighting you, not here. But what I do want is for you to leave my family alone. As far as I'm concerned, you are a non-entity in Emily's life. If it was up to me, she wouldn't even be allowed to listen to your music."

"What I don't get is why."

Mike shrugged and straightened the wrinkles Seth's grip had made in his linen shirt. "Does love have to have a reason? Emily's my daughter."

"Hello?" The voice belonged to Abby.

As the front door clicked closed, Carolann called, "I'm in the kitchen, dear."

Seth ground his teeth together. What was she doing here?

At the pocket doors, Mike glared over his shoulder at him. "I won't let you hurt Emily or Abby. They've both been through enough."

He squared his shoulders. "Who said I had any intention of hurting anyone? I just want what I've been denied."

Mike slid the doors open, and Abby looked through the opening. Her eyes narrowed and she stood straighter. "What are you doing here?"

He pushed past Mike into the foyer. "Wow, I feel so welcome."

"Mom! Did you see who..." Emily ran down the hall from the kitchen. "I guess you did." She looked from her mother to Mike to him, her expression falling and taking on the pucker of confusion. "What's going on? Why do y'all look so mad?"

Mike smiled and draped his arm around her shoulders, pulling her into his side. Something in Seth squeezed and the acid in his gut churned when Emily met Mike's gaze with trusting eyes only a daughter could have for her father.

"Nothing." Mike glanced at Abby. "I didn't expect your mother, that's all." The obvious lie seemed to slide easily off Mike's tongue.

Emily rolled her eyes. "Right. The wicked witch might not like it."

"Emily," Abby said in an exasperated tone, "please, don't speak about Tammy Jo that way. She's your stepmother."

Seth clamped down on his teeth so hard pain shot through his face. Obviously, Tammy Jo hadn't changed much in the intervening fifteen years since he'd left town. He wouldn't have his daughter mistreated by anyone.

Mike's jaw worked as if he had to unlock it to get the words out between the compressed line of his lips. "Tammy Jo is doing her best, sweetheart. Give her time. Now, let's go have dinner."

Mike's arm remained wrapped around Emily's shoulders as he led her down the hall. Abby fell into step behind them, and Seth followed.

Frank and Tammy Jo greeted him with a welcome that surprised him, after the chilly response he'd received from his old-time best friends.

Mike moved around the large glass-and-wrought-iron table. Letting go of Emily's shoulders, he pulled out a chair for her to sit, then helped Tammy Jo into her seat. He sat between his wife and Emily.

Seth pulled out a chair and raised a brow at Abby.

"Thank you," she murmured and slid into the chair.

Carolann brought a platter of thick steaks to the table. He helped her into her chair, and she smiled at him as he took a chair between her and Abby. "My, what a gentleman you've turned into."

"You taught me well. What else can I say?" He looked around at the food in the middle of the table. "Everything smells delicious, Carolann."

She waved his compliment away. "Frank, why don't you pop the cork on that fancy bottle of wine Seth brought with him? We'll save Tammy Jo's wine for the next time."

Frank retrieved the bottle from the kitchen. He held the bottle up upon his return to look at the label.

Tammy Jo's eyes brightened the moment she saw the bottle. "Tahbilk Shiraz. I'm impressed. Wish I could drink some," she said, looking across the table at him. "You have good taste."

He shrugged and unfolded his brightly colored napkin in his lap. "I like good wine."

"I hope you didn't pay an arm and a leg for it. I told you we were just having steaks." Carolann picked up the salad bowl.

"I think I can afford it."

"I saw *Forbes Magazine* just ranked you at the top of its richest country singers," Emily said, and he met her awed gaze.

Swallowing hard, he shifted in his seat and shrugged. "Don't pay too much attention to those reports."

Carolann passed the salad bowl to Tammy Jo, who filled her plate and passed the bowl to Mike, then looked across at him again. "I saw you in Dallas in March. What a show! I couldn't believe our very own Seth Kendall could sell out an entire football stadium."

He turned to take the wine from Abby. When his fingers brushed hers, awareness zapped through him. He held her gaze a beat longer than necessary.

She blinked and let go of the bottle. If he hadn't hustled to hold on, the hundred-dollar wine would have slipped out of his numb fingers and landed on the concrete floor of the patio.

"Thanks. This past year was amazing." He glanced at Tammy Jo as he poured the wine into his glass.

"What's it like being so rich and famous?" Emily took the salad bowl from Mike and dumped a pile on her plate.

His tongue felt heavy and dry. "I guess it's fun, though I don't like the lack of privacy sometimes. People always want to know what's going on in your life when you're famous. Like that *Forbes* article. Why would it matter how much money I made? The music I play should, which is the reason I can fill stadiums and sell millions of records." He shifted in his chair again and looked around the table. Every eye was pinned on him, and he quickly averted his gaze to his plate.

Abby took the salad bowl from Frank and put a small amount from it on her plate. When she passed the bowl to Seth, she was careful not to touch him. Had she felt the same electricity he had the last time her fingers brushed his? "But just think what you had to give up to play that music and make those millions."

Her quiet words hit him like a punch. Yeah, he knew what he'd given up. But she hadn't given him a goddamned choice either.

Before he could respond with something he could say aloud, Emily asked, "Do you have any favorite singers?"

He pulled his gaze from Abby to Emily. She pushed her salad around on her plate as a soft blush colored her cheeks.

"Yeah, I have my favorites. But there are too many to name." He tried to clear the lump from his throat. It didn't work. "I'm influenced by a lot of different singers and styles."

"Do you ever listen to other kinds of music?" She looked up from her plate with big green eyes so much like his own, his chest tightened. How could no one else see the resemblance?

He shrugged and picked up his fork. "You can't be in this business unless you do. I love all kinds of music, though country is what I do because that's what I am. What kinds of music do you like, sunshine?"

Abby caught his eye, and he held her gaze. Something deep and bruised filled the brown depths.

"There isn't much that I don't like either." Emily's lips curled into a small smile. "I'll listen to anything. That drives Daddy nuts." She playfully poked Mike in the arm with her elbow. "He doesn't have much appreciation for different kinds of music."

Mike put his fork down and bumped her shoulder with his. "No, I guess I don't. But then, I don't consider half of what's on top forty radio music anyway. Whether they call it country or otherwise." He looked across at Seth and picked up his glass of water. "I never understood how you could want to be a country singer, but would turn my stereo as high as it would go and jam out with Kiss or Michael Jackson."

"I remember," Abby said with a wry grin. "I never quite got that either."

"I prefer classical and jazz. Mike hates my music too." Tammy Jo patted Mike's forearm. "Don't you, cupcake?"

Cupcake? Seth hid his grin by stuffing salad into his mouth.

"I don't hate your music." Mike grinned at her. "Sweetpea."

Emily made gagging sounds, and they all laughed--except for Mike and Tammy Jo. Frank cleared his throat and raised his eyebrow at the lovebirds, but Mike and Tammy Jo clearly were thinking about other things.

Seth glanced at Abby. She'd tucked her chin and smiled. Not the response one would expect from the jilted wife. He leaned back in his chair. What the hell really went on fifteen years ago? Maybe his aunt knew something.

Emily brought him out of his thoughts. "Do you know everyone in the music business?"

He shook his head and shifted forward to pick up his fork again. "Of course not, but I'd like to think I have a lot of friends in Nashville. Country singers usually stick together. Oh, there're feuds now and then, but it's been said that those of us in county music are like one big family."

"I noticed your guitar by the door..." Emily's bright, hopeful eyes left no mistaking the unspoken question.

"Yeah, I thought after supper we could play a few songs together."

"Oh, that would be wonderful." Carolann clapped her hands together.

"I thought you had something to do." Mike glared and squared his shoulders.

"Nope." He smiled and picked up his wineglass. "I'm all yours tonight."

"I propose a toast." Tammy Jo stopped him, before he could take a sip of the wine. She raised her glass of apple juice.

Mike all but scowled at her. "Whatever for?"

She smiled and glanced at her husband. "To good fortune, of course."

Abby lifted her glass of wine and looked across her shoulder at him. "Sounds good to me."

"To good fortune, then." Touching her glass with his, he smiled. He had a feeling her idea of good fortune wasn't the same as what he had in mind.

* * * *

Abby had long ago lost her appetite, but she'd managed to force some salad and half a steak down her throat. She hadn't wanted to come to dinner at the Ritters'. Tammy Jo always had a way of making her feel unwelcome in the house she had always considered home. She'd only come to appease Carolann.

Now, she understood why her ex-mother-in-law had been so adamant for her to show up. Seth was going to be here. In Carolann's way of thinking, it was a reunion between three old best friends.

She put a glass into the dishwasher and turned to take the plates Seth rinsed in the sink. "I want you to keep this sing-a-long short."

He wiped his hands on a towel, leaned his backside on the edge of the island, and crossed his arms below the rolled up sleeves. She tried not to notice the way his white western shirt stretched over his broad shoulders, or how the muscles bunched in his arms. "Afraid the Ritters might figure out your little charade if they see us together too long?"

She glanced around and kept her tone low as she closed the door of the dishwasher and set the dial. "No. You forget that my father was Irish. Mike and I had explained away Emily's coloration a long time ago."

"Well, wasn't that convenient."

She felt his gaze boring into her back as she picked the dishcloth out of the soapy water in the sink.

"Why didn't you ever tell the Ritters the truth about Emily?" His voice rumbled through her, low and determined.

"Mike said it would be better for everyone if we kept the truth secret." Unable to meet his gaze, she busied herself with wiping the counter.

Seth moved to stand over her. "But you aren't so sure that was a good idea."

She set the dishcloth on the countertop and faced him. "I never set out to deceive you or anyone else. But neither do you have a right to come in here and destroy Emily's life, or mine. Mike Ritter is the only father she knows. He's the only father she's ever had."

He leaned in. His lips were close enough to kiss, and his scent of sandalwood and something exotic enveloped her, taking her back to that night on the beach. His eyes flashed with the dangerous fire of his temper. It was similar to the flame of the passion she'd once seen in the green depths. She didn't expect or want the heat curling in her belly, and shivered with a sudden and fierce desire.

"I'm her father, Abigail. I wanted to be her father after she was born. It was you and Mike who insisted I had no business messing things up."

"I never said any such thing. You never tried. You just left."

He pounded a fist on the counter top so hard she jumped. "Yes, I left! I wasn't welcome at home. Dad ran me off with a shotgun. Mike wouldn't even let me see my daughter. He made it quite clear you and he were happily married, and I had no place in your life. I was under contract to be in Nashville to start recording my first album."

What did he mean, Mike wouldn't let him see Emily?

Before she had a chance to voice her question, his eyes darkened as the pupils dilated, obscuring the stormy green. "But I'm no longer nineteen and scared shitless. I could make things very rough for you and this fantasy you've got working."

A cold lump quickly replaced the tangle of heat in her belly. "What-what do you mean?"

He backed off and tapped the countertop. "I'm talking a custody battle. I could have a judge order a paternity test. I think we both know the media hoopla the results would cause."

Her heart slammed into her chest wall. "You wouldn't do that."

"Try me. Now that I've met Emily, I want to get to know her." He walked over to look out the kitchen window. The hard line of his jaw melted, and he swallowed so hard his throat moved up and down. "I was a fool when I let Mike talk me out of being in her life after she was born."

"What do you mean?"

He glanced at her. "Don't pretend you don't know."

The strings of guitar music provided a soft counterpoint to the hard tension in the kitchen. Emily was outside on the patio playing around with her guitar, waiting for them to finish with the dishes she and Seth had insisted on doing.

"All I want is to have some time with my daughter. That's all I'm asking for." When he looked over his shoulder at her, sadness replaced the anger in his eyes. "I'll keep your little secret. I'll just be her favorite singer. The family friend who made it big in Nashville. I don't want to hurt her. As much as it galls the hell out of me, I see what Mike means to her."

He moved toward her and shoved his hands into the pockets of his jeans. "Besides, I don't want to hurt Carolann or Frank any more than you do." He glanced outside again, his voice husky as he spoke. "But I'll sue you if I have to."

A part of her wanted to give in to him, but a larger part wanted to punish him. Let him take her to court; she'd make sure the world knew what kind of jerk Seth Kendall really was.

She gritted her teeth and fisted her hands by her sides. "I'll let you have tonight, Seth. But don't ask for more."

She turned away and strode through the French doors.

Chapter 3

Seth stared at the scribbled numbers on a page of the small notebook he carried around with him. He didn't go anywhere without a notepad with a stubby pencil stuck through the spiral. He never knew when he'd be inspired with an idea for a song. However, these weren't the words of the next song to win a Grammy. Written here was the phone number for the only woman who had ever haunted his dreams.

Closing his eyes, he remembered the night he'd left the woman he loved standing on her porch, and driven away.

He hadn't intended to leave. He'd made up his mind he'd forfeit his place in the talent show. Do what was right, what his father would have expected of him. He'd marry Abby and raise his baby.

But when he'd arrived at Abby's house, fear gripped him. He loved her, but how did he know if it was enough? His mother had given up a chance at fame when she got pregnant with him. She'd married a man she didn't love, who didn't believe in her, and it ruined her. She'd turned to booze and drugs and hated his father and him.

But what if he didn't turn out like her? What if he turned out like his father? Mean and hateful. Abusive. He'd never dream of hitting Abby or their baby, but what if he lost his chance at doing the one thing he loved doing? What if he ended up trapped here, on the ranch, just like his mother? According to his grandfather, she'd hated the bar scene, the county fairs and rodeos. With her talent, she'd deserved so much more than singing to drunken cowboys. What if he was reduced to that? Would he become the worst of both of his parents?

Abby deserved better than a mean drunk for a husband. She'd spent the last five years dealing with her father's alcoholism and bad temper.

There was only one option.

"Come with me," he pleaded, wrapping his arms around himself to ward off the pain stabbing his heart.

"I can't. How can I run off with you? I have the ranch and Daddy to take care of."

"We'll be back, Abby. It's only five months. Then if--when--I win, I'll have to do a tour. But we can come back here after that. You'll have the baby, and I'll have my record deal. Surely, someone in your family would take care of the ranch. Or we could just hire someone."

Her eyes glinted in the moonlight as if she would say yes. That she'd agree to go. Turning away, she hugged the porch post. Her soft voice sawed through his hope. "Seth, I can't leave. We both know it would never work. Besides, Daddy's dying. He has brain cancer."

"Abigail..." He touched her shoulder, but she flinched away and faced him.

"We don't love each other. Not like that. It was..." She looked away and sniffed. "It was just sex. You know...you were the only boy I ever kissed." She averted her eyes and gave a half shrug. "Things just got out of hand. Now, I have to live with..." She sniffed again as if holding back tears.

He grabbed her shoulders and gave her a little shake. "I don't believe that bullshit. I..." But he couldn't say the words; he couldn't tell her he loved her. Not with her shaking her head.

She closed her eyes and took a deep breath before looking at him. "You go and do what you have to do. We'll be fine. I have my inheritance. My baby will never want for anything. But I can't be a part of your life. Seth, I don't love you."

He let go of her as he stared at her, and his heart shattered into a million pieces. "I'll be back, Abby. I won't leave you. I'll help take care of the baby."

He opened his eyes and stared at her phone number. He'd kept his promise, but when he'd returned seven months later, she was married to someone else.

She'd loved someone else.

And his baby became someone else's.

He flipped the cardboard cover closed on the pad and tossed it behind him onto the full-sized bed. Seth rubbed his hands over his face and stood. Instead of sleeping, he'd spent the past six hours staring at the ceiling.

The light coming through the lace curtain stabbed through his head like a hot knife. He blinked a few times and stumbled to the antique armchair in the corner of the small bedroom, muttering, "I wasn't even drinking and feel like shit."

He rummaged through the clothes he'd tossed in the duffle bag until his fingers closed around the bottle of aspirin.

In the bathroom down the hall, he downed three of the pills with a glass of water. As he stepped out of his shorts, he turned on the shower.

Feeling somewhat human again after washing away the sleepless night, if not the pain from the memories, he reentered the bedroom. Crammed with antique furniture, the small room served as his aunt's guest room. He'd spent many nights in this room after Johanna would take him away from John when the beatings got too bad.

The notebook lying on top of the patchwork quilt drew his attention as he pulled on a pair of jeans. Carolann had given him Abby's phone number before he left the ranch last night. He should have known she was playing matchmaker.

Seeing Abby again had sent him spiraling. He'd thought he'd finally gotten over her.

How wrong had he been?

No other woman had ever left her imprint on him as Abigail Crawford had. He'd had more than his share of flings and one-night stands. They'd meant nothing to him. He had no lasting memories of any them, not even Amanda Lang, who was the closest thing to a steady girlfriend he'd ever had.

With Abby, he could remember everything.

He finished getting dressed, and headed downstairs. He still had to talk to Johanna about what she knew about Abby and Mike's relationship.

And what she knew about Emily.

His heart ached every time he thought of the baby he'd been denied knowing.

He shook the recurring thought from his mind, but couldn't shake off how he felt about Abby and what had happened.

Had that one incredible night by the lake been enough to purge him from her system? Probably. However, she was still deeply embedded in his.

He found Johanna on the back porch of her modest two-story house. Flowers of every color and variety filled the small backyard and hung in overflowing pots from the beams of the overhang. The sweet perfume of the flowers mixed with the earthy richness of dew-covered soil and recently mowed grass.

She poured water into a massive hanging begonia and smiled at him as he carried a cup of coffee with him through the screen door.

The sun peeked over the tall, white painted fence. A dog barked down the street and the kids next door called goodbye to their mother as they headed out the door to catch the school bus.

He sipped the strong brew, suddenly glad he'd let his aunt talk him into staying with her instead of the hotel in town. "I can't believe you still have this huge garden to take care of."

Johanna set the watering can on the banister. She wiped at her brow under a big straw hat with the back of her hand, then went about pulling faded flowers off the monster plant. From the dirt clinging to the knees of her jeans, she must have been pulling weeds in her garden. And it wasn't even seven AM yet. "Remember when I'd drag you out here to help me in the garden?"

He chuckled and leaned against the railing. Bringing him to her home had been her way of getting him away from his father's abuse. She'd stood up to her twin more than once. Her threats of going to the law or taking him away from his father would stop the belt-whooping for a little while, until he did something to piss his father off again. "I remember. I had a terrible time remembering what was a weed and what was one of your precious flowers."

"But you learned quickly. You actually liked coming here eventually." She smiled and glanced at him. "Do you still like to garden?"

Gardening? Hell, he barely remembered what his perfectly manicured lawns even looked like. He shrugged and glanced into his cup. "No. I leave that to my groundskeepers."

"Ah. Of course." She snapped off a few more buds.

"What the heck do you feed those things to get that big, anyway?"

She tossed a handful of dead flowers into a bucket. As she propped her hands on her still-slender hips, she faced him. "Okay, out with it. I hate this damned beating around the bush, and you know it. How did dinner at the Circle R go last night?"

"Good." How was he going to ask what he wanted to know?

"Was Abby there?"

He met his aunt's bluebonnet blue eyes and let out a long breath. "Yeah." He motioned with his hand to one of the white wicker rockers. "I need some information. But first I have a confession to make."

She sat in the chair, folded her hands in her lap, and waited for him to spill his guts.

As he stared at the mug hugged by his hands, he jumped in to the muddy waters of confession headfirst. "The night Dad and I fought about me sneaking off to Amarillo to try out for *America's Rising Star*, I did something..." He cleared his throat and sipped the cold coffee.

"By the way you're stalling, I'm beginning to think you killed somebody."

He looked across at his aunt rocking slowly on the chair and spewed the truth. "Emily Ritter is my daughter."

She didn't stop rocking. Her face didn't even register surprise. Johanna simply nodded once then met his gaze. "Did you just figure it out?"

Sitting up, Seth felt the tension knotting his shoulders relax a little and then get tighter. "You knew?"

"Pretty hard to miss it. She looks too much like my momma."

Setting his mug on the side table, he stood and leaned over the banister between two of her monster geraniums. "Who else knows?" The ceasing of the creaking of the rocker against the floor alerted him when she stopped. He looked over his shoulder at her. "Did Dad know?"

"If he did, he never let on. And I'm sure some of the people who knew Momma wonder, but not many of them are still alive." She narrowed her eyes at him. "You never answered my question."

"No, I didn't just find out." He stared over the back yard again without seeing it. He sighed and tucked his chin, feeling suddenly ashamed. "I knew Abby was pregnant when I left."

"What are you saying, Seth Christopher? That you left that poor girl and ran out on your responsibilities? I know damned well your daddy raised you better than to do something like that."

There was no mistaking the condemnation in his aunt's voice. He turned, ready to defend himself, but how could he argue against the truth?

No, he wasn't going to feel guilty about leaving. He'd had no choice. Abby hadn't given him one.

"I wanted to take her with me, but she wouldn't come. I promised her I'd be back." He fisted his hand against the sudden knots into which his guts were tying themselves. Obviously, they protested this kind of spillage. "But when I came home, she was married to my best friend. In some ways, as much as it hurt, I was also glad."

Johanna sucked in a breath. "You were afraid of becoming like your parents."

He nodded and closed his eyes against the ache. "I was stupid. I was a fool. But yes. How could I think anything else? Mom was nineteen when she screwed up her chance at Nashville by getting knocked up with me. Then committed suicide when she couldn't stand life on the ranch anymore. Dad used his belt or fist whenever he didn't get what he wanted from me. Great role models, those two."

"Why didn't you ever come home?"

He stared at the profusion of colors in the garden and sighed. "Abby and Mike were happy, or at least seemed to be. And I knew I'd never be half the father Mike would be. He convinced me Emily would be better off never knowing me." He faced his aunt and fisted his hands against the pain in his soul. "And like a damned fool, I believed him."

"You don't believe that now, do you?" She stood and came up beside him. Her touch was warm and gentle as she laid her hand on his bare forearm.

"No."

"What are you going to do?"

He shook his head and tightened his grip on his fist until his hand cramped. "I don't know. I told Abby I'd sue her for custody, but I'd really hate to do that. It would only end up hurting everyone I care about--my family, Frank, Carolann, Emily...Abby."

Sucking a breath into his tight chest, he forced his fist to relax and stabbed all ten fingers into his still-damp hair. He met her sympathetic eyes and let out a breath along with his anger. "I made a terrible mistake, but I'm a whole lot older and wiser now. I want to get to know my daughter. I may never be able to be her father, but I want her to know me...not just what she reads in the tabloids. Me." He tapped his chest to emphasize the word. "Because Abby and Mike don't seem to think I deserve even that right, I need to be armed with as much information as possible."

"What kind of information?"

Seth turned his body and leaned his backside against the banister. "What do you know about Mike and Abby's marriage?"

"You're expecting me to know about that?" She arched an eyebrow and went back to pulling dead flowers off the King Kong-sized begonia.

"You must have seen or heard something. You and Carolann are friends." He crossed his ankles and hooked his thumbs in the belt loops of his jeans. "What happened to them?"

She snorted and tossed handful of faded blossoms into the bucket. "What you really want to know is how the heck he ended up with Tammy Jo?"

He smiled and shrugged one shoulder. "When I left for Nashville, he and Tammy Jo were gaga for each other. When I come back seven months later, he and the mother of my baby are married and in love. I don't know about you, but something just isn't adding up."

She studied him a minute, then began removing dead flowers from one of the geraniums next to him. "Tammy Jo did leave for Harvard before Mike and Abby married, if I remember correctly. Maybe they broke up and he moved on."

"To a girl pregnant with his best friend's baby?"

She stopped snapping faded stems from the plant and leaned against a porch post. "All right, here's what I think."

She tossed her hat onto one of the rockers and narrowed her eyes at him. The morning sunlight caught in the bright red of her graying ponytail and made her appear at least twenty years younger. Why hadn't Johanna ever married?

"Charles Crawford was dying. It was only a matter of time. Abby was his only heir. I heard a rumor that she inherited not only the ranch but nearly five million dollars from that big insurance settlement Charlie won after the accident that killed Emmy and paralyzed him."

A frown tugged on his brow. He knew about the money Abby's father won after a drunk driver ran the only red light in town and hit the passenger side of the car Charlie was driving, killing his wife instantly and leaving him with a broken back. "Charles died right after Emily was born, didn't he?"

Johanna nodded and compressed her lips. "Yeah, she was born in the spring, I think, Charlie passed away in the fall. But I remember John commenting on something that Frank had told him. Mike insisted on paying off some of the debt on the Circle R. If he hadn't, the Ritters would have lost that place. Since the Crawford ranch sits next to the Circle R, I think Mike planned to join the ranches someday. But when he and Abby called it quits two years ago, he gave her back her ranch."

He snorted and looked out over the backyard. "Did he give back her money, too?"

"That, I don't know."

He peered at her again. "So, when did Tammy Jo show up in the picture?"

"Not long after Abby and Mike divorced, they started coming out at town functions together." Johanna plucked more dead flowers off another hanging plant. "That was when Mike ran for sheriff. She supported him, and well, we all know the power the McAllisters yield in this town."

He studied her. Her lips still compressed together, and by the way she was attacking the purple trumpets of the petunia, he feared for the poor thing's life. "You have an opinion about all this."

She paused, but didn't look at him. "I don't know a blessed thing, but I'll say this." She met his gaze with blazing certainty belying her words. "I think Mike and Tammy Jo have been together ever since her father died four years ago when she came home from New York."

"Well, isn't that interesting."

She peered down her finger at him, reminding him of when she was his sixth grade teacher. "Not as interesting as why you aren't trying to make things right. Just remember, you can catch more flies with honey than you can with vinegar."

What the hell did that mean? "I have every intention to make things right, Aunt Johanna. I think that's one reason I came home. I realized how much I've missed. If Dad left me the ranch, I'm moving onto it. I'll be away much of the time, but this will be my home."

"This has always been your home, Seth." Her finely lined lips curled upward as she crossed the porch. She opened the screen door and paused. "You really should get your butt over to the nursing home and visit your granddaddy."

The door closed with a bang, leaving Seth staring after her. What did his grandfather have to do with anything?

* * * *

Abby pulled the crazy flamingo-themed lab jacket over her hot pink scrubs as she entered the dementia and Alzheimer's unit nursing station from the staff lounge. Behind the communal desk, fellow RN Jenny Lynn Cooke sat working at the computer.

Jenny Lynn stopped typing and looked up when Abby stopped beside her. "Hey. I guess Darlene called off again. You're stuck with an agency nurse tonight."

"Yeah, I know." She picked up a clipboard. Scribbles of the latest orders from the doctor covered the front page. "We'll get along fine. She's coming on right before supper and the evening meds rodeo." When she finished reading the orders for her shift, she sighed and looked over the charts lying on the desk.

"Darlene hasn't called me. How's Max?" Jenny Lynn asked, referring to Darlene's husband.

She leaned against the edge of the counter and looked down at her hands. Jenny Lynn and Darlene had been her friends since nursing school. Since Darlene was married to a Hispanic and Jenny Lynn didn't have a prejudiced bone in her body, she felt blessed to have them as her friends. She never had to make excuses for her parents' mistakes. "Max took a turn for the worse after she got off work last night. He had a terrible seizure and slipped into a coma."

"Oh, no." Jenny Lynn covered her mouth with her hand. "That's not good."

"No, it's not." She'd become a nurse because she hated the cancer that finished rotting what was left of her father's brain after years of alcoholism. "Between Dad's brain cancer and the years I worked at the hospital, I've seen my share of glioblastoma patients. Personally, I'm surprised he's hung on this long."

A masculine--and painfully familiar--voice drifted from behind her. "I'm sorry, Miss, but I'm looking for Mr. Steven Harris's room. The receptionist downstairs said he was on this floor."

She turned to the man on the other side of the counter.

"Abigail? You work here?"

"Yes."

"Oh my God! You're Seth Kendall." Jenny Lynn gasped, jumping from her chair, and gaped at him.

Seth dragged his gaze from Abby and addressed the other nurse. "That would be me. My grandfather is Steven Harris."

Blushing, Jenny Lynn regained her composure and smiled as she held out her hand. "I'm terribly sorry. I shouldn't be surprised. He has pictures of you in his room. I've just never met anyone remotely famous before. I'm Jenny Lynn Cooke and am one of the nurses taking care of Mr. Harris."

"It's okay, Miz Cooke. I haven't met many nurses either."

Jenny Lynn giggled as she took her hand back. "I have all of your CDs and really love your last song on the radio. The lyrics are just crazy."

He chuckled, the deep rumble warming her clear through.

"Thanks," he drawled. "I usually don't choose that kind of beer drinking, tongue-in-cheek song, but I liked it when I heard the demo."

The corridor filled with the nursing staff poking their heads out of rooms. As fans descended upon him, he lowered his head. "Thanks. I do appreciate your support, and I'll see what I can do for y'all."

For several minutes, Seth signed autographs and chatted with the staff as if they were the most important people in his life. Taken aback by his sincerity and genuine appreciation of his fans, Abby watched him, as enthralled as her co-workers.

Eventually, the staff went back to their duties, and the few patients who had come forward to see about the ruckus forgot he was even there.

"Sorry, ladies. Sometimes things get a little wild." Seth flashed a lopsided grin.

His gaze traveled over her face and hair, lingering on her lips. Heat crept over her cheeks. She tugged the jacket closed and crossed her arms over her chest. Nothing was as asexual as her whimsical, baggy scrubs and the stethoscope looped around her neck.

"This was so nice of you." Jenny Lynn held her autographed day planner in the air. "Thank you."

"You're most welcome, Miz Cooke." He studied Abby a moment. "Can I talk to you later?"

The deep green of his shirt was the exact color of his eyes. The reddish blond hair she'd always loved curled around his ears and over his collar.

"I'm sure I'll be busy." She forced herself to look down at the clipboard and away from his eyes. Her heart raced and sweat gathered on her neck. "Seth, what are you doing here?"

"Visiting my granddaddy." She didn't need to look at him to hear the smile in his voice.

"Right," she muttered and picked up the clipboard, but set it back down again when it quivered with her trembling hands.

Jenny Lynn said, "I can show you to his room if you'd like."

"Thanks. But since Abby doesn't seem to be busy right this minute I'll just talk to her now. We grew up together and were good friends."

"You never told me that you knew him personally."

She shrugged, not wanting to think about just how personally she knew Seth Kendall. "My ex-husband and Seth were best friends when we were all kids. I was kinda the tag-along. Our ranches all border each other."

Something unreadable passed over his eyes as they bore into hers, but he covered it with another mega-watt grin. "Then I left town and Abby married my best friend."

Jenny Lynn glanced at her, and Abby read the question in her eyes. Jenny hadn't missed the undertone in his voice, but covered it by smiling again at him. "It's been a pleasure meeting you, Mr. Kendall. I'm sorry about your daddy."

"Thanks for your kind words, Miz Cooke."

Jenny Lynn gathered her things. "See you later, Abby. Hope they all behave for you."

"Have a good night, too, Jen."

Jenny Lynn moved through the door into the staff lounge, then he said, "So, where's Emily while you're working here?"

He sucked the air right out of the room. Although she'd never wanted to see him again, she'd often wondered how the experience of being near him would affect her. She didn't like the effect in the least.

She stared into those fathomless eyes. She'd drown in them again if given the chance. He had a power over her. Despite his betrayal, she wanted to feel the breathless, frantic passion she'd felt that night on the beach.

Damn, she had to get a grip. He didn't want her, and she sure as hell shouldn't want him.

"She's with Mike this week." She busied her hands with rearranging the charts on the desk. "He has joint custody of her."

"Doesn't sound like she likes Tammy Jo." Seth leaned on the top shelf surrounding the counter.

Finished with rearranging the charts, she braved another look at him. Big mistake. Why did he have to be so sexy? "Emily is a fourteen-year-old girl who doesn't understand the adult world."

"Meaning she blames Tammy Jo for breaking up you and Mike. But what Emily doesn't understand is that he started cheating on you four years ago when she came home."

His words caused her belly to do a somersault. How had he figured it out so easily? She narrowed her eyes on him and moved out of the station as another nurse entered. She wasn't about to have this conversation now or ever. "Follow me. I'll show you to Mr. Harris's room."

He smiled at the other nurse before following her away from the station. "Thank you."

She led him down the wide corridor to a private room at the end of the hall. At the door, he gripped the frame and turned toward her. "I'd like to come over to your place tomorrow. I promised Emily I'd go riding with her."

She stepped away and looked over her shoulder at him. "I'm not so sure that's a good idea. She already idolizes you. I'd hate for her to get hurt when you leave."

"What if I don't plan to leave?"

"You will. Emily will be busy tomorrow. 'Bye, Seth."

* * * *

Abby quick-stepped it down the hall, and Seth followed the swish of her long, glossy braid as it moved with her, brushing the top of the curve of her perfect ass. He wanted to run his fingers through all that luscious hair and caress all those wonderful curves. How could any woman look that sexy in that God-awful pink getup?

He tapped the doorframe with a fist and fought the fire roaring through his veins.

They'd see about him leaving. But not before he got to know his daughter.

Entering the room, he frowned at the utilitarianism of his grandfather's space. He sent his mother's brother money to make sure his grandfather had a private room, but even so, it wasn't very homey. His first mentor sat in a faux leather chair staring out the window into the gray sunlight.

Seth sat in the chair opposite him. "Granddad?"

There was no recognition in his brown eyes when Granddad looked at him and smiled. "How's it goin'? Do I know you?"

"Yeah, Granddad, it's Seth."

"Uh, that's good." He looked back out the window. "I was hoping to see George today."

George? Ah...his great uncle who had died in World War II.

"He'd promised to come by and take me fishing this afternoon."

He wasn't sure what to say, so he sat there and didn't speak at all.

Granddad studied him and pursed his lips. "I wish I knew who you were. You're such a fine young man. But I'm tired now. I think I'll go to bed." He pushed on the arms of the chair, but fell back into the seat.

Seth went to him and supported his weight around his waist. Steven Harris had once been a rodeo champion when he wasn't playing guitar and singing with his family band. He broke broncos and wrangled bulls.

His heart twisted at seeing the once-proud man so frail. "Let's get you into bed, Granddad."

The old man smiled at him and patted his hand with one crippled with arthritis and wrinkled with age. "I wish you could stay until Suzie comes home. She'd like you."

He stopped dead in his tracks. Wednesday, during the funeral, had been the first time in years he'd given his mother much thought. He swallowed hard. "Suzie was my mama, Granddad."

A deep frown pinched his wizened forehead, and he shook his head. "Not possible. She's just a little girl. What kind of trickery is this?" He struggled against him. "Get away! Get away! You're like the rest of 'em. Get away, I said!"

"Granddad, it's me, Seth. You taught me how to play guitar when I was ten. Don't you remember?"

"No!" The old man shook his head, and as tears came to his eyes, flailed at him. "Get away!"

"Please, Granddad, calm down."

Afraid he'd fall out of bed, Seth held onto him, instantly worsening the situation. Over his shoulder, he called toward the open door, "Nurse! Nurse, I need help!"

A middle-aged woman dressed in light green scrubs rushed into the room and pressed a button near the bed. She took over holding the hysterical, fragile man. "I'm sorry, Mr. Kendall, but you'll have to leave."

He nodded, backed toward the door and stared at his grandfather as the nurse cooed soothing words. A moment later, Abby rushed past him with a hypodermic needle in her gloved hands.

She glanced over her shoulder at Seth, then gave his grandpa an injection, speaking in a soft, calming voice and holding the old man's hand.

His grandfather calmed down, and Abby came to stand beside him. "I gave him a sedative. He'll go to sleep now and will be back to what's normal for him in a few hours."

He dragged his gaze from the bed to meet her brandy eyes as she washed her hands at the sink by the door. "He doesn't even know who I am. The last time I saw him was about three years ago in Austin. He remembered me then."

She motioned for him to move through the door. When she took a breath, her smock top tightened over her breasts under her jacket. "Alzheimer's is a difficult disease. It steals a person's memories, his life, and confuses and saddens his family. Some days he remembers, but mostly he regresses into the past and is oblivious to anything current. Eventually, he won't even remember the past."

"He was talking about wanting to go fishing with his brother George. What upset him was when I told him I was Suzie's son. He thinks she's still a little girl."

"I know it's hard to understand, but when he's stuck in the past, it's better to go along with him."

"You mean pretend I'm someone else?" As they moved down the wide corridor, he looked around at the patients wandering the halls. None of them paid them much attention.

"No, not exactly. Just don't try to force who you are on him. That's what upsets him. He feels like you're trying to trick him."

They stopped at the nursing station, and she went behind the desk. She leaned over the keyboard and began typing. He stood on the other side of the counter and stared at her. He'd just witnessed a side of Abby he'd never seen before. She'd always been so shy and unsure when they were growing up--a byproduct of being called names until he and Mike put a stop to her tormenters. But now, she exuded take-charge confidence.

"You're very good. I couldn't take care of people like this."

Without looking up at him, she said, "My first job after nursing school was in the ER. After a year there, I moved to the ICU." She met his eyes and the corners of her lips turned upward. The sight of that first smile hit him in the chest and sent a jolt straight to places better left forgotten. "Mike calls me a freak because I enjoy high-stress jobs."

"Who took care of the ranch, your daddy, and Emily?"

"What?"

"While you went to nursing school? Wasn't your father and the ranch the reasons you couldn't go to Nashville with me?"

"Not that it's any of your damned business." Abby looked at the computer screen. "I went to school after Daddy died. Emily was in preschool, and Mike had finished up with the police academy. We hired a manager to run both the Circle R and Crawford Creek."

He forced his jaw to relax. The last thing he wanted to do was sue Abby for his rights. It would be a tabloid feeding frenzy if it got out that he had a teenage daughter. He also had no desire to hurt Carolann and Frank--or Emily. Which suing Abby for custody would definitely do.

Just remember you can catch more flies with honey than you can with vinegar.

If he wanted to get close to Emily, he had to first get close to Abby.

Smiling at this new angle, he reached into his back pocket and retrieved his wallet. She glanced up as he jotted a number on the back of a business card. When he held it out to her, she stared at it for a moment.

He chuckled. "It won't bite, I promise. I'd like you to give this to whoever arranges activities for the residents and staff here."

"Oh?" She took the card, read the information, and then met his eyes.

"The front of the card has my manager's and agent's numbers. What you'll need is my cell number on the back. Have the activities director give me a call by Wednesday."

"Why?"

"Because I'd like to put on a private show for the folks and staff of the home to personally thank y'all for the work you do."

While she pocketed the card in her jacket, he donned his hat. Turning on the charm he knew worked on the ladies, he drawled, "Goodnight, Abigail."

He turned and moved down the hall toward the elevator with a swagger he'd long ago learned women enjoyed watching. At the elevator, he glanced back at Abby and grinned when he caught her staring. Tipping his hat, he entered the car and lost the smile.

So, they were still attracted to each other.

What could he do with that?

By the time the elevator doors opened on the first floor to greet a bunch of surprised nurses, he'd found his smile again.

"Howdy, ladies."

He could do a hell of a lot with Abby's attraction.

If he was willing to risk his heart.

* * * *

Seth strummed a melody on his guitar and sang a few words. "Well, that sucks."

He looked out over the river and thought about the words a moment. This time when he sang the words with the melody, he liked the phrasing and jotted it in his little notebook.

The horse he'd ridden to the riverbank whinnied, and he looked behind him. Squinting against the blaze of the late morning sun, he peered to the east. A rider and horse were making their way up the southern bank of the Salt Fork.

He stood, set his guitar against the rock he'd been sitting on, and stepped out from the shade of the live oak. He'd come out to the Double K early that morning. Johanna wanted him to go to church with her, but he wasn't ready for that much immersion into the community of McAllister.

Although he avoided entering the house, he liked to take one of the horses and ride over the ranch. Today, he'd brought his guitar. He only had a few months to start writing songs for his next album, and the lazy river bordering the north side of the ranch had always provided great inspiration when he was a teenager.

When the rider silhouetted by the sun came close enough for him to make out who it was, his heart skipped a few beats.

Emily approached at a trot. As she stopped next to his gelding, she smiled brighter than the sun riding the sky above her. Her long ponytail flamed under the brim of her cowboy hat, making her appear ethereal.

"Hi," she shyly said as she dismounted the big sorrel. Her worn boots hit the hard dirt and sent up a cloud of dust. She was a regular little cowgirl angel.

His little cowgirl angel. The song he was struggling with suddenly flew out of his mind as an even better string of lyrics and melodies played in his mind.

He swallowed hard and found his voice. "Hey, sunshine. Nice morning for a ride."

She looked around and nodded. "Yeah. I like to ride along the river."

"Your mom know you're down here?"

She nodded and tucked her hands into the back pockets of her jeans. "I like to ride after we get home from church." Jutting her chin toward his guitar, she asked, "I thought I heard music."

He glanced at the instrument. "Yeah, I'm writing a new song." As he stuck his thumbs into his belt loops, he faced her again. "Or at least I'm trying to. It's not going very well. Do you write?"

She blushed and averted her eyes. "A little, but I'm not any good."

"Can't be as bad as my first attempts. I actually wrote a song about that rock and tree over there." He pointed to the boulder his guitar leaned against and the tree shading it.

She laughed and folded her arms loosely in front of her. "You're kidding."

He shook his head and grinned. Good, she'd seemed to relax a little. "Nope. I was about thirteen, I think. I'd written a lot of songs while sitting under that tree."

"How long have you been out here?"

Shrugging, he lifted his hat and wiped at his forehead with the back of his hand. "Since about eight, but I think I may soon head back. I forgot how hot it gets in August."

The heat had nothing to do with his nerves and the sweat gathering between his shoulder blades.

Her smile sagged a little. "Oh, I probably should be going then. I'll see you around."

She turned to mount her horse.

"Emily." She looked back at him. He rubbed his goatee and cleared his throat. "I said soon. Not now. Want to sit with me for a little while? Maybe you can help me with this crazy song. I'm having trouble with the chorus."

A blinding grin replaced her frown. "You want to write a song with me?"

"Yeah. Let's see what we can come up with."

Time seemed to fly as he picked out the melody on the guitar and sang what he had already. She sat on the ground by his feet and patted her thigh with the beat. She'd add a word here and there, or make suggestions about phrasing, once she'd lost her shyness.

They struggled with the last line of the bridge. Nothing Seth came up with matched the meter he'd set for the song. She hummed the bridge a few times. Frustration furrowed her brow. "It's almost there."

"Here." He unclipped his guitar strap and handed the instrument to her. "Play it and see if that helps."

Her eyes widened as she stared at him, then at the guitar. "You're gonna let me play your guitar?"

Shrugging, he looped the strap around her neck. She gingerly took the one-of-a-kind Gibson as if it were the most precious thing in the world. He smiled and clipped the strap to the neck. "Yep. Because you're gonna help me get this danged thing done."

Her freckled face shimmered as she strummed down the strings. She looked up at him.

Would she feel the same awe when she found out he was her father?

Dear God, the tight squeeze in his chest was back. Her very existence sent a thrill through him every time he thought about it.

Emily studied the strings a second, then played and sang the song from the beginning. She glanced at the notebook and hummed the end of the bridge where there needed to be words to finish the thought. Then she sang,

"*Flowers fade, seasons change,*
But I'll always be traveling the long road home."

The tingling in his chest was back. "That's perfect.

The whine of an engine invaded the peacefulness. As the noise grew closer from the east, their horses lifted their heads from grazing and perked their ears.

Seth stood and looked down the riverbank. The sun had long ago climbed the sky and clouds moved in to cover the blue expanse. He glanced at his watch. Shit, it was well past one. The driver of the Gator didn't surprise him.

Abby stopped in the middle of the trail and marched toward them. She glared at him, then turned to Emily. "Do you have any idea what time it is? I was worried sick."

Emily glanced at him and carefully slipped the leather strap from around her neck. "I'm sorry, Momma."

"I lost track of time. I'm sorry you were worried." He took the guitar from Emily and held it in one hand.

Abby huffed out a breath and headed toward the Gator. "C'mon, Emily, I have things I need to get done."

Emily gave him a small smile, but her eyes held disappointment. "I had fun today."

"Me too." He patted her shoulder and jutted his head toward her horse. "Why don't you ride back with your mom? I'll follow behind with your horse."

She glanced at Abby, who sat stick-straight on the worn seat of the dust-covered cart with a motor. When Emily met his gaze again, she nodded. "Okay."

A half-hour later, he rode out of the pasture behind Abby's barn, led Emily's mare into the stable and unsaddled her. He searched until he found a brush, then rubbed the mare down and gave her a ration of oats in a bucket. He let her out into the pasture as Abby marched across the driveway toward him.

Damn, did the woman ever just walk? He rested a hand on the doorframe above his head and waited for her to unleash the storm brewing in the clouds swirling in her eyes.

She pushed past him into the relative coolness of the barn and turned to face him. Her fists were propped on the curve of her hips. His gaze stuck on the cutoff denim shorts and the long toned legs below the frayed edges. Her tennis shoes were set apart in a tense stance.

He dragged his eyes back up her body and smiled. Her soft curves were a welcome treat when compared to the supermodel walking skeletons he normally hooked up with. "You know, time has definitely treated you well."

Hell, he hadn't intended to put voice to the thought.

When she narrowed her eyes into flashing slits, he would've sworn he heard thunder roll somewhere over the prairie beyond the river. "I told you to stay away from Emily."

He dropped his hand from the frame and tucked his thumbs into his belt loops. "What do you think was going on out there? Some clandestine meeting?" Forget it, the calm and cool way wasn't going to survive this storm. He dropped his hands to his sides and took a step toward her. She glared up at him, and he peered down at her. "I was already there. She rode by and stopped. I am sorry you were worried, but damn it, I didn't do anything wrong."

"She said she helped you write a song."

"Yes. She helped me salvage a song I was about to give up on. Our daughter has talent, Abby."

She looked past him, stepping closer. "She isn't your daughter."

"I never signed my rights away and I never will. Remember what I said. All I want is to get to know my child."

Before she could say anything else, he walked out of the barn and mounted his horse. Storm clouds had rolled in within the past forty-five minutes and the thunder was coming closer.

He'd have to haul ass to get back to the Double K before the heavy gray clouds let loose their fury.

As he cut across Abby's pasture to the old trail leading to the Double K, he thought of the awe in Emily's eyes. Something had to give, or the storm he'd unleash by going to a lawyer might lay waste to more than just the land.

Chapter 4

Seth paused on the road and looked up at the wooden arch proclaiming the name of the ranch in bold black lettering--a *K* with another *K* formed from the bottom leg. The name of the thousand-acre ranch came from his great-great-grandfather, Christopher "Kit" Kendall.

Live oaks lined up along the drive like guards raising their sabers to form an arch. His mother had felt like a prisoner here. Would he too, if he inherited the ranch? As he got closer to the house, a weight settled on him. He'd never wanted to be a rancher. Could he seriously be considering becoming one now? As he looked over the house and the pastures around it, he wanted this place more than anything.

Or did he? Was it really the ranch he wanted, or just a sense of having a home? Of being part of a family?

The white clapboard two-story house with dark green gingerbread trim and louvered shutters didn't offer any answer. He and Abby had often sat on the swing hanging from the porch rafters, pouring out their frustration over their troubled young lives.

Abby.

Since his two run-ins with her over the weekend, he couldn't stop thinking about her. He looked to the east. Her three-hundred-acre ranch bordered the Double K. Next to her was the Circle R. After the accident, which took her mother's life and left her father wheelchair-bound, Seth's father had offered to buy Crawford Creek. But Charlie Crawford had refused to sell because thirteen-year-old Abby wouldn't hear of it. She had always loved that place.

He was glad she got the ranch back as part of her divorce settlement. The Ritters hadn't deserved the ranch any more than John Kendall had.

He parked beside Judge Ritter's pickup in front of the detached garage.

Stopping at the front door, he took a deep breath and pulled the hat from his head. When he couldn't stall any longer, he rang the doorbell. A moment later, Johanna opened the door.

She smiled and moved back, allowing him entry. "I wondered if you were going to show up."

He stepped past her into the entry and checked his watch. "You told me ten o'clock. It's ten o'clock. I'd call that being right on time." He leaned toward her and kissed her cheek. "But I'd bet my record deal if the old man was here, he'd be hoping I wouldn't show up."

Johanna stiffened and stepped away with a disapproving frown puckering her brow. "Seth Christopher, that is no way to talk about your dead father. God rest his soul."

He shrugged and looked around the entry. A curved oak staircase wound up to the second floor. The morning sun blazed through the windows and glared off the faded floral wallpaper.

With a sigh, he shifted his hat from one hand to the other. "Maybe not. But I can't help but feel that way. He ran me off with a shotgun when I came home after getting my record deal. Made it pretty clear he hated me."

She wrapped her arm around his waist and started moving toward the study. Outside the door, she stopped and met his gaze. "Seth, John loved you. I know he hurt you, and I'll never fully forgive him for the way he treated you. But there are things involved that he never quite resolved in his own head."

Snorting, he looked down at his hat. "He wondered if I was really his kid because Mom cheated on him the same time she got pregnant."

She sucked in a breath. "How do you know about that?"

"So, it's true?" He snapped his narrowed gaze to lock on hers. "I thought maybe it was a dream. I overheard Mom and Dad fighting the night before she died, but I sometimes don't know what's real and what I've imagined since then."

Johanna tightened her hold on him and stared up at him with eyes swimming in tears. One slipped past and rolled down her pale, finely lined cheek. "Yes, there was a time right before she died, he wondered because he found out Suzie had been with someone else."

"Who was he?"

She looked away and closed her eyes. Another tear slipped past.

"Jesus." Clarity jolted through him. "She was with someone you cared about?"

Opening her eyes, she nodded. "Yes. My husband. But you don't belong to Buck Tomlin."

He couldn't have been more shocked than if a bull had mauled him right here in the house. Johanna had been married to the fiddle player in his grandfather's band--his mother's band?

She squeezed him in her one-armed hug as he swallowed hard. "You have to understand, Suzie never wanted to live here. Your grandfather insisted she marry John when he found out she was pregnant."

"When did Dad find out about her and Buck?"

She glanced at the back of her left hand. Was she imagining her wedding band? "The day before she died. John found a letter Buck had written in answer to one she'd sent to him just days before her wedding. She wanted him to come forward and claim you as his baby so she could get out of marrying John. But he refused because he swore he couldn't make a baby--which I'm about a hundred present sure he couldn't. At least, I never got pregnant during the two years we were together. We divorced the year you were born. Mainly because I found out about his affair with your mother--along with other women. But I never told John about him being with Suzie. I knew it would have broken his heart."

She used her free hand to wipe at the tears. "John was ten years older than your mother. The Harrises never had much, and I think Steven hoped marrying her off to someone like John would calm her down. John was determined to make something of this ranch and have a family. He knew she was a wild one, but he loved her. So, he married her."

"Maybe she wouldn't have been so wild if he'd allowed her follow her dreams."

She slowly nodded. "John, I'm afraid, was a fool. He thought if he kept her here, she'd learn to love him."

"Instead, she hated us both," he murmured and lowered his head. How could this all still hurt so damned much?

She shook him and glared at him with a blue fire of conviction. "Don't you dare talk like that. I was never a fan of your mother. Quite frankly, I hated her. Suzie hurt my brother, but she loved you. If she hadn't, she would've left."

She did. She committed suicide. He glanced at the wood-paneled door of the study. Moving out of her embrace, he opened the door. "Let's get this over with. I have a meeting with the nursing home director later."

The study was as he remembered it. The shelving along one wall held various books about ranching, leather- and paper-bound ledgers and journals of the ranch, dating back to 1878. The family Bible was displayed on a table beside an old leather wingchair that had sat in front of the tall window for a hundred years. The unforgiving space reeked of musty books and Cuban cigars--just like the man who had lived and died in this room.

Frank Ritter stood behind the desk and held out a shaky hand to him. The judge had come down with Parkinson's Disease during Seth's senior year of high school, which hadn't helped the Ritters' financial situation.

He greeted Frank, then turned to Tucker and Vince Cowley and shook their hands in turn. Their parents had lived and worked on the ranch while they were growing up. Presently, Tucker was the acting manager of the place, and Vince was a foreman.

"Shall we get started?" Johanna took her seat beside Seth's chair.

"Yes." Frank adjusted his reading glasses and cleared his throat. "As all of you know, John Kendall was one of my oldest and dearest friends. Not much unlike you, Seth, and my son, Mike."

The judge gave him a sad smile, and Seth looked away as bitterness swamped him. *No, you wouldn't have betrayed Dad the way Mike did me.*

"So, years ago when John asked me to read his will, I said I would but never dreamed it would happen so soon. I'll miss him." Frank's hand violently shook as he opened the folder before him, and he swallowed hard enough to make his Adam's apple bob up and down. He readjusted his glasses and read the will.

"To my son, Seth Christopher Kendall, resident of Brentwood, Tennessee, I hereby bequeath stock of which the current market value equals over two million dollars. He may take any items he desires from the residence."

Clearing his throat, Frank pushed his glasses into place again after his shaking jiggled them down his nose. He furrowed his brow as he read.

"The property known as the Double K ranch, including the livestock, equipment, and business assets, is to be sold at fair market value."

Frank looked over his wire-rimmed glasses at Seth.

"The moneys from this sale will be set up into a trust fund for the minor child hereafter referred to as Minor Child."

Johanna grabbed his hand, but Seth didn't feel her touch. He was too numb. Although Frank continued reading, his words stopped registering.

His father had made sure he could never come home. Unless he paid for it.

"Who?" Johanna asked, interrupting Frank's reading and breaking into Seth's thoughts. "Is the identity of this minor child ever named?"

"I'm sorry, Johanna, all John indicates is that this beneficiary will remain unidentified until such time the minor reaches the age of eighteen."

"He doesn't say who it is? How can that be? You wrote the damned will! This land should go to Seth."

"I'm sorry, but I didn't write it. John had a lawyer over in Amarillo write it up. I'm as curious as you are about his secrecy, but John never did anything without a good and sound reason."

"Is this binding?" Seth fisted his hands where they lay on his thigh. Why the hell did he care so much? "Can I contest the will because of this unusual secrecy about the minor?"

"Sure, but I think it will be fruitless. The lawyer in Amarillo holds the identity of the anonymous minor benefactor in counsel. It is completely legal. Unorthodox, but legal."

Frank turned back to reading the rest of the will, bequeathing a portion of John's wealth to Johanna. The Cowley brothers were to each receive a year's severance pay and a sizable inheritance for their loyalty.

As soon as the judge concluded the reading, Seth was on his feet and heading for the door. Only Frank's calling his name stopped him.

He lifted the leaf of the folder before him and held a sealed envelope over the desk. "Your father wanted me to give this to you."

Dad, you're as much a prick now as you've always been. Seth contemplated the letter a long moment before taking it. "Thanks, Judge. I'll be seeing you around. Aunt Johanna, I'll see you back at your house."

Without looking back, he donned his Stetson and left. Once in the SUV, he tossed the letter onto the passenger seat.

He pounded his hand on the steering wheel. Of course, his father would do something like this. Anything to keep him from his birthright.

Johanna rushed off the porch and stopped at the open window of his SUV as he turned the key in the ignition. "Seth, wait! Where're you going?"

He sucked in a breath between his teeth and cut the engine. "First, to my meeting and then home. I'm going back to Nashville. Maybe there really isn't anything here for me."

Johanna waited until the Cowley brothers passed by. They tipped their hats at him and his aunt, but none of them said anything. What was there to say? As soon as the place sold, Tucker and Vince would be out of a job--and homeless. This place was as much their home as it was his.

"If you leave, you really are a damned fool. Listen to me. I know this hurts. Get out of there and let's talk about what I think is going on."

He pounded the steering wheel again and opened the door.

She moved back as he got out, and pointed toward the yard. "Let's go back to the gazebo and get out of this blasted sun."

He followed her through the recently mowed grass to the grove of pecan trees and the gazebo. The fresh scent of cut buffalo grass mingling with the heat of the day normally would have relaxed him. Not today. He was wound so tight he thought he'd explode.

Once inside, Johanna sat on the swing and patted the space beside her.

Seth shoved his hands into his pockets and leaned a shoulder against a post. "What's there to say? Dad hated my guts."

"No, he didn't." She slapped her jeans-covered thigh. "Who do you think this minor is?"

He shrugged and stared out over the pasture. "Maybe he has a bastard out there somewhere."

"Jesus, you are every bit your father's son!" Her sharp tone along with her use of the Lord's name in vain caused him to snap his head toward her. "Think!"

He puckered his brow, until the answer hit him square in the chest so hard he flopped down on the bench beside her. "Emily?"

"Yes." She sighed and patted his hand where it rested limp on his leg. "He probably figured out the truth the same way I did. She looks like our momma." She smiled and shrugged. "Which probably also put his mind at ease about you being his son, by the way."

He met her gaze, and she squeezed his hand. "John couldn't put Emily by name in his will. Hell, maybe he wasn't even sure Abby knew you were her father. Or that you knew. And he wouldn't want to hurt the Ritters, but he wanted to provide for his granddaughter in some way."

She sighed again and looked down at her hand on his. "He couldn't trust that you wouldn't sell the ranch just to spite him. At least this way, the profits go to Emily. She'll need the money more than you do."

He looked past her at the pasture. Cattle lazily munched on grass, swishing their tails at flies. He felt like one of the flies--unwanted and unloved. "What should I do?"

She patted his arm and stood. "If I have to tell you that, you're as useless as teats on a bull."

Chapter 5

"Wow, this place is hopping tonight," Jenny Lynn said as she smiled at Earle, the bouncer, after she and Abby and entered Gatlin's Friday night.

Earle shrugged a big shoulder and spoke loudly to be heard over the band and the crowd. "It's always busy Friday nights. You ladies know that." He smiled at Abby. "You gonna do some dancing?"

"If the right cowboy asks, I will." Abby gave him her best flirty smile. "See you around, Earle."

Jenny Lynn leaned over and said near her ear, "He's sweet on you."

She laughed and shook her head. "Jenny Lynn, Earle Murphy is my second cousin. I'm an Indian. I'm not from West Virginia."

Jenny Lynn looked over her shoulder at the bouncer. "Shoot. He's cute."

"And big and twelve years older than me. If and when I decide to start looking for a man, I won't need any help. C'mon. There's a table near the dance floor. I know you want a clear line of sight to the band."

Jenny Lynn waved at the drummer, who winked at her.

As they sat, she looked at the band. She set her phone on the glossy top and pulled her hair over one shoulder. "So, Wayne Cover is the reason you just had to come to Gatlin's tonight. I can't believe you're dating him again."

Jenny Lynn shrugged and waved at a waitress dressed like a cowgirl in tight jeans, red western shirt and boots. "What can I say? He's got so much going for him. He's a Texas Ranger and hot as a devil. Besides, it's not as if we're serious. He likes me for my blond hair and big boobs, and I like him for his big... Well, I think you get the picture."

Abby couldn't fight the blush burning her cheeks. She'd known Jenny Lynn for eleven years and shouldn't be surprised by anything the woman said. She glanced at the man she'd never wanted to imagine without his clothes. His buzz cut seemed at odds with the way he played the drums. "Yeah, I get the picture better than I'd like to."

Jenny Lynn ordered them both longnecks. Once the waitress left, she leaned over the small round table. "So, when was the last time you were on a date?"

"I'm not interested in dating. I have Emily to consider. The divorce was tough on her."

The waitress dropped off their beers, and Jenny Lynn thanked the girl. She took a sip and set the bottle on the table. "Yet, not six months after said divorce was final her father remarried."

She picked at the label on her bottle. "It's different for a man. You know that."

"All I know is you are in some serious need of loosening up. And it wouldn't hurt for you to get laid while we're at it."

Before Abby could wrap her tied tongue around an appropriate comeback, a commotion at the front drew her attention. Seth Kendall stood inside the door talking to Earle, while a dozen or so people--mostly women--flocked to surround him.

"Now, there's a man who's dream worthy," Jenny Lynn said just loud enough for Abby to hear. "I still can't believe you know him."

"Yeah, I know him." *And yes, he's definitely dream worthy. Just don't fall in love with him because then he becomes a nightmare.*

"He sang here while he was in high school, didn't he?"

She chugged half her beer and nodded. "Every Friday night for about five months before his father found out. He was only seventeen at the time. Earle would let Mike and me sneak in just to watch him." Her heart raced at the memories. "He sure was something."

Still is.

A woman pushed her way to the front of the pack to stand before Seth. Her tight, orange tank top barely covered her large breasts.

"Oh my God! I can't believe I'm finally meetin' you!"

Abby winced at the shrillness of the woman's shriek.

Jenny Lynn laughed. "Leave it to that floozy to make a scene."

He seemed to switch on the charm with a blazing smile.

"Can you sign my shirt?" the woman yelled.

Before Seth even requested it, the woman produced a Sharpie. The band ended their song. For a moment, the place was quiet. He took the marker and asked, "Thanks. What's your name, darlin'?"

"Mindy Lou Watson. Put it here." She pointed across the tank top over the swell of her left breast. "Right over my heart."

He glanced around, and when his gaze snagged Abby's, smiled. He signed his name as Mindy had requested. "There you go."

"Oh...Oh! This is amazing. I absolutely love you! I want to have your babies!"

Before she could throw herself at him, Earle came forward. "Mindy Lou, that's enough." Then he waved his hands to the horde, motioning them to move out of the way. "Let's give Mr. Kendall some room."

"Oh, Earle, you ain't no fun," Mindy Lou whined, but she and the rest moved out of the way.

With the mountainous Earle leading him, Seth headed toward their table.

"Sweet mercy!" Jenny Lynn looked at her with her mouth hanging open. "He's headed our way."

He stopped at their table and grinned at Abby for a long moment before glancing at Jenny Lynn. "Hello, ladies. This seat taken?"

Jenny Lynn gestured to the chair. "Uh... No, it's not. Please join us."

Abby's heart stopped before starting again. He removed his hat and set it on the edge of the table as he pulled out the chair. Once seated, he ran his hand through his hair. Her fingers suddenly itched with the forbidden desire to do it again. Talking about Jenny Lynn's sex life reminded her exactly how non-existent hers was.

She needed another drink. Her mouth was as dry as West Texas during a drought. She waved down a waitress and ordered another round for them.

Jenny Lynn picked up a peanut from the bowl in the center of the table, but put it back as if she decided eating peanuts was forbidden in his presence. "Is it always like that?"

Seth laughed and waved at a few more people around them. "In another half hour, this place will be a fire hazard."

"I'd hate that. You can't go anywhere, can you?"

He brushed his thigh against Abby's knee when she shifted in her seat. The action sent a jolt through her. And from the way his pupils dilated when he looked at her, he felt it, too. She stilled and willed her body not to respond to the naked heat in his eyes. It didn't work any better now than it had Sunday when he stood in the doorway of the barn, as sexy as a cowgirl's wet dream, and blatantly undressed her with his gaze.

"It does get tiresome, but really it's not crazy all the time. I'm a local boy who's famous. I expected it to be like this if I came in here."

The nervous server brought their beers. Jenny Lynn leaned on her elbows and grinned. "Just think, you missed out on a marvelous opportunity with Mindy Lou."

"What's that?" He picked up his beer.

"She wanted to have your babies."

"Thanks, but no thanks. I think I'm good." He laughed, but it sounded hollow.

The darkening of his eyes caused quivers to dance over Abby's skin and settle low in her belly. Her hand shook as she lifted her beer to her lips and gulped.

Jenny Lynn looked from her to Seth and pushed back her chair. She stood and picked up her first beer, leaving the new one Abby had ordered. "I'll see y'all around. The band's finishing this set, and I'd like to see Wayne before he has to go back on stage.

For a moment after Jenny Lynn left, Seth sipped his beer and stared at Abby. The last notes of the old George Jones hit seemed to hang in the air between them.

"The band's good."

She nodded and rubbed her sweaty free hand on her jeans and gripped the frosty bottle of beer with the other. "Yeah. They play here just about every Friday night. The lead singer is Christy Gatlin's husband, Clint Grier. He's one of Mike's deputies. The other two playing guitar also work for the sheriff's department, and the drummer is a Texas Ranger out of Amarillo. The keyboardist is a volunteer firefighter and the female backup singer works in the DA's office. The band goes by the name Lawman. They're really popular around here."

Before she rambled off anything else he hadn't asked for, she finished her beer and reached for the one meant for Jenny Lynn. No use letting it get warm. Wayne could buy Jenny's next drink.

"I guess I better not cause any more trouble tonight. I wonder how many times they've arrested the audience."

She set the bottle down. Seth had always had the ability to make her smile no matter how worked up she was. "I don't know. But I'm sure it has happened a time or two."

"So, where's Emily tonight?"

She sighed and looked around. Most of the patrons were still watching them. It was like being in a dream in which she'd left the house naked and hadn't realized it until too late. Her palms were clammy and her throat was dry.

Because telling him Emily's whereabouts were none of his business would only make a scene, she sighed. "Sleeping over with a friend. Birthday party."

He took another slow drink from his bottle. "Seems to me she's with other people more than she's with you."

She straightened her spine and clenched her beer bottle. "Emily is fourteen and is one of the most popular girls in school. She's a junior officer in 4-H and has recently started barrel racing. She's in the marching band, school orchestra and sings every chance she gets--school, church, fairs. Not to mention, she plays softball and is on the track team. No, she isn't home much, but what would you know about her life? I doubt you even remember her birthday."

The flame in his eyes dimmed, and he lowered his head. His voice dipped so low she had to strain to hear it over the din. "March twenty-third. I've given her a gift every year."

"What?"

Regret clouded his green eyes. "I've given her something every year. For her first birthday, I bought her this big old teddy bear." He held out his hands to demonstrate the enormity of the thing. "But I chickened out and never sent it to you. I still have it back in Nashville."

He took a swig of his beer and swallowed much harder than the liquid required, if the movement of his throat was indication. "Since her second birthday, I've deposited ten thousand dollars in a savings account for her. I put in another ten grand every Christmas and five at Easter."

She leaned back in the chair and stared at him. "That's twenty-five thousand dollars every year?" she managed to squeak out after she got her mouth to work.

"Not to mention the trust fund I've already set up for her." He smiled and lifted his beer in the air. "With the millions she'll get out of the sale of the Double K and my contribution, Emily will be quite a wealthy woman when she turns eighteen."

She must have heard him wrong. "What do you mean by the sale of--"

"Hello, Seth. It's been forever and a day." A very pregnant woman dressed in a maternity version of the honky-tonk uniform took that moment to approach their table.

"Christy Gatlin?"

She grinned and nodded.

He stood and gave Christy a long hug. "You're all grown up. And pregnant!"

Christy patted his arm. "I couldn't wait to grow up and marry you. I had such a shameless crush on you when you'd sing here. I still do. But don't tell my husband."

"Don't tell me what?" Clint Grier came up behind his wife.

Christy looked over her shoulder and shrugged. "Nothing, honey. My favorite superstar and I were just catching up."

"Trust me, sugar, he'd return you. I'm the only one dumb--I mean--in love enough to put up with you." She glared at him while the rest of the rest of the group gathering laughed. With a broad smile, Clint held out his hand to Seth. "Seth Kendall, it's a real pleasure to finally meet you."

"Thanks. You're pretty good up there."

"Thank you." Clint actually blushed. "Christy's dad never stops talking about you."

Abby heard the voices and watched their interaction, but her mind was stuck on Seth's last words. What did he mean by the sale of the Double K?

Seth turned as Jimmy Gatlin rushed through the staring crowd. The large man laughed, cuffed him on the shoulders and wrapped him in a bear hug. "By God, boy! You sure as hell did it up right. I knew you would. I just knew it! It's so good to see you."

Seth pursed his lips. "You always had faith in me."

A hush fell over the barroom as everyone hung on the exchange between Seth and the man who had given the superstar his first singing gig. Even Abby watched the exchange, forgetting her questions about what he'd meant.

"Thanks, Jimmy. I'll never be able to repay you."

"Well, I know talent when I see it." Jimmy huffed and jerked a thumb toward his son-in-law. "With this fool behind me, I mostly take pity on him and his band of scalawags. Maybe, you'd be willin' to show 'em how it's done..."

Jenny Lynn gasped from where she stood beside her boyfriend as the question hung in the air.

Seth grinned and looked around at the band. "Oh, I think they do fairly well on their own. But I wouldn't mind sharing the stage with them, if y'all are agreeable."

Clint's mouth fell open, and when he closed it, he nodded. "That would be the opportunity and the honor of a lifetime."

For a little while, they all chatted and caught up on Seth's success and Jimmy talked about how talent was harder to come by these days.

"I'm sorry about your daddy." Jimmy patted Seth on the shoulder again.

Seth nodded and that brought the conversation to a stop.

"Christy, make sure they get a round of beers and a basket of wings on the house." Jimmy smiled at them as he nodded and moved away.

Jenny Lynn went off with the band. Abby knew what her friend was doing, but didn't say anything; doing so would make things worse. Jenny Lynn wouldn't understand why she was fighting the sparks between them.

Once they were alone, she asked, "What did you mean about Emily being a wealthy woman?"

He tapped his fingers on the table. "Dad's will reading was Wednesday. He wants the ranch sold."

Her heart started beating faster. If the ranch was sold, he wouldn't have a reason to stick around.

Why didn't that prospect make her happier? That was what she wanted, wasn't it?

He met her gaze. "The money from the sale is to go into a trust fund. Although the kid wasn't named in the will, Johanna and I are fairly sure it's Emily. She'll get the money when she turns eighteen. Which is how I have my fund for her set up."

"Wait, Johanna knows about us? About Emily?"

"Yes. She actually figured out Emily was mine a long time ago. Probably Dad did too."

"How?" The word came out choked on her dry tongue. The rushing blood in her ears suddenly drowned out the noise around them.

He finished his first beer and shrugged. A smugness filled his eyes. "She looks like my grandmother--with a lot of you mixed in."

"Dear God," she breathed and looked down at the table.

Christy brought them the round of beers and the basket of buffalo wings Jimmy had ordered.

Abby pasted a smile on and thanked Christy, then picked up her latest beer and drained over half of it.

"Whoa. You should probably go a little easy."

She sat the bottle on the table with a thunk. "Right."

The buzz hit her like a punch in the head. She wasn't used to drinking and that was her fourth beer in less than an hour. She closed her eyes to keep the room from spinning.

She blinked and met his gaze. "What do I have to do to make you go away?"

A corner of his very kissable mouth curved up. "Go out with me?"

"Excuse me?"

"You heard me. C'mon, Abby. What would one date hurt? You and me. No talk of who betrayed whom. There was a time we may have had something special going on."

She shook her head. Big mistake. She blinked and willed her vision to clear. "That was a long time ago."

"Yes, it was. I'm not going to be in town long. But I can promise you I'm not staying away this time. I'll be back."

"Why?"

"You know why. Abby, I have no intention of telling her I'm her father, but you can't keep this secret forever. The day she turns eighteen she'll receive two letters informing her she's my daughter. Don't you think she'll be angry that you refused to let her get to know me?"

He was right. Emily would hate her for the deception. But how could she hurt her family by revealing the truth? Mike asked her not to say anything, and she owed him that much after all he'd given up to marry her- -to become her daughter's father. He didn't know about this development. Telling him wouldn't be easy.

She had to eat something. The room spun around her. She sprinkled Tabasco sauce over the wings and nibbled on one of them.

Seth lifted his beer to his lips and winced. "How can you eat those things with hot sauce all over them? If I remember Jimmy's wings, they're already hot enough to peel the paint off the walls of hell."

She delicately licked her fingers. "I'm half Apache. My mother used to eat jalapeno pepper jelly every day on toast. I like hot things. It's in my blood."

Seth drank his beer as she ate the spicy chicken. "I'll remember that," he said in a voice that did funny things to her already uneasy stomach. He stood and leaned over her. Next to her ear he whispered, "Don't let the Tabasco warm you up too much. I'll be back."

She trembled as he strode away in tight black jeans making him look like sin on legs. Maybe he was right--she should leave the Tabasco alone. Mixing it with beer was probably not a good idea anyway.

He conferred with the musicians for a few moments, then went outside with Earle and returned with his guitar case. Jenny Lynn informed her she was going home with her Texas Ranger drummer. "God, he's so psyched about playing for the great Seth Kendall."

"You seem a little psyched yourself."

She grinned and hugged Abby. "I'm in for a hell of a ride tonight when we get back to his place. You'll be okay getting home?"

"Yes, I'm fine. Be careful."

Jenny Lynn winked and walked toward the stage. She kissed her drummer, and he got onstage.

The crowd cheered and gave Seth a standing ovation as he took his place on the stage. She joined those standing.

Regardless of everything, she loved Seth's voice and listened to his music all the time, but she hadn't seen him perform live since he'd left. While they were growing up, they'd sit on the old porch swing at the house or in the gazebo on the Double K, and he'd play his guitar and sing to her.

Her first kiss came after he'd sung an old Alabama song to her in that gazebo. The sparks they shared had scared them both. Considering with their next kiss three years later, she'd ended up pregnant at seventeen, it was probably a good thing. She'd never wanted anything but success for him--until the day she peed on a stick and stared down at a bright pink plus sign.

What would have happened if he'd stayed around? Was he right about the talent competition being his best chance at success? What would have happened if the fear of being alone hadn't forced her hand and she hadn't married Mike?

Seth had succeeded. She'd always known he would, and her heart swelled with pride. Tears gathered at the corners of her eyes as he walked over to the stool before the mic. He belonged up there.

She'd never share her real reason for not going with him that night. Hadn't he realized America might not have fallen in love with a young cowboy from the Texas Panhandle if they'd known he had a pregnant teenage Indian girlfriend? But she'd never dreamed he wouldn't write or call. That he'd completely ignore her after he left Texas.

"We don't love each other. Not like that. It was--it was just sex. You know...you were the only boy I ever kissed. Things just got out of hand. Now, I have to live with..."

"I don't believe that. I--"

She shook her head, not wanting to hear what he had to say. The pain in his gaze broke her heart. She closed her eyes and took a deep breath to give her the strength to tell the biggest lie in her life up to that point. "You go and do what you have to do. We'll be fine. I have my inheritance. My baby will never want for anything. But I can't be a part of your life. Seth, I don't love you."

Her words came back to haunt her. She stared at him on the stage. What had he been going to say to her? That he loved her? That he wanted to marry her?

Had she broken his heart as badly as she had her own?

He peered at her, his eyes burning with an emotion she couldn't name-- no, she wouldn't name it. When he looked down at his guitar, a soft smile touched his lips. He hid most of his face under the brim of his hat.

The crowd settled as the band took their positions behind him. Seth pushed his trademark black Stetson back on his head and locked his gaze on Abby.

"I'd like to thank every last one of you. I can't begin to tell you how much y'all mean to me. I wouldn't be anything without y'all."

His voice was husky, and he readjusted his guitar strap around his neck. "When I was seventeen, Jimmy Gatlin asked me to sing on this stage. All I had was my mother's old acoustic guitar. It was enough, I guess, because Jimmy kept telling me to come back." He paused and bowed his head as the audience erupted with applause and whistles. When he looked up, he smiled and winked at Abby. "So, here I am again with my biggest fan from then in the audience."

Although the passion of the crowd swept her away, she didn't miss the play of emotions on his face. She understood what he hadn't said, that there was as much pain in the memories as there was joy of those early years. John Kendall's lack of pride in his talent had hurt Seth deeply.

John had come to every single football game in which Seth had played quarterback and every fairground rodeo in which he'd roped calves, but his father had never wanted to hear him sing. As far as she knew, John hadn't seen his son sing before an audience.

When he strummed the opening to one of his early hit songs, she was as captivated as everyone else in the honky-tonk.

Seth's soulful voice spoke of love and loss, and she got lost in the words.

He seduced the entire room with his whiskey-smooth voice, and he pulled at the part of her soul that had always belonged to him. He couldn't be more than a memory, but she sniffed at the burn in her sinuses as she wished Seth Kendall could be more.

Only a Memory wound down to the mournful accompaniment of the steel guitar, and he captured her gaze over the distance, singing only to her.

He'd written that song about her! Being thrown at full gallop couldn't have jolted her harder. She gasped and leaned back in her chair.

Still dazed by the revelation, she couldn't concentrate on the final four songs he performed. How many of his other songs were about her? The thought rattled her. She ordered another beer, and still her throat burned. Her mouth was dry.

Why hadn't she figured it out sooner? *Only a Memory* was one of her favorite songs.

Probably because it resonated with her about him too.

The set finished, and he thanked the band for their backup. He walked off the stage to another standing ovation, rowdy applause, whistles and catcalls. Seth regained his chair beside her and took a long draw on a glass of water a waitress had brought him.

Mischief glimmered in his green eyes as he grinned. "So you just now figured it out?"

"I never realized that song was about me."

He sipped his water and watched her. "A few of my songs are about you."

She didn't want to consider the possibility she'd inspired any of his songs. Most of his love songs were about lost or unrequited love. What did he really want from her?

She had to get away from him. Had to escape or she'd do something stupid and destroy her family. There was no doubt she wanted him, missed him, was lonely, and she was drunk. An extremely dangerous combination.

"I need to go home." She wobbled to her feet and took off through the crowd toward the exit.

"Abby?"

She didn't stop, but rushed out the swinging doors.

At the door of her Silverado, he caught up and took her arm. "You aren't in any condition to drive. Where's your friend?"

She shook her head. "She's going home with--with her boyfriend." He was right; she was too drunk to drive home. Tears threatened to fall, and she swallowed her pride as she fell into his arms. "Please, take me home."

Chapter 6

Seth helped Abby into the passenger's seat of her Silverado and buckled the seat belt. She closed her eyes and swayed to the left. The dim light coming in from the streetlight shimmered in her dark glossy hair as it slid over her face. She pushed it back and blinked her eyes open.

"You gonna be okay?" He couldn't resist smoothing the silky mane away from her face.

She nodded and swallowed. "I will be once I'm home." He moved to close the door, but she reached out to stop him. "Wait. My phone. It was lying on the table."

"I'll get it." He closed her door and took a deep breath. The last thing he wanted to do was walk back into that bar, but he had to arrange for his SUV to be delivered back at Abby's place.

He entered, and Earle stepped in front of him. "Is Abby okay?"

Nodding, he rubbed his goatee. "I'm going to drive her home. Can you arrange for my Escalade to be taken out to Crawford Creek tonight?" He opened his wallet and pulled a fifty out. "I'll make it worth the trouble."

Earle held up his hands and shook his head. "I ain't taking your money. I'll get your rig out to the ranch."

"Thanks, Earle." With a smile, he put the bill away and handed him the keys to his SUV.

"You just take good care of my cousin. She's had a hard life. Growing up half Indian wasn't hard enough, but she practically had to raise herself in the bargain."

He nodded and glanced toward the table they had occupied earlier. Another couple sat there now. "Hey, Abby left her cell phone on the table. Was it turned in at the bar?"

"I'll check." Earle made his way toward the crowded bar.

He shoved his hands into his pockets and shifted his feet as he tried to ignore the curious stares. Jenny Lynn weaved her way toward him. He pulled his hands from his pockets and squared his shoulders.

"Where's Abby? I've been looking for her."

"She's not feeling well, so I'm taking her home. But she left her phone."

Jenny Lynn held it out to him. "Here. I picked it up and was going to give it to her."

"Thanks." He had a feeling she had something more to say by the way her gaze slid from his and she crossed her arms.

"Abby will kill me if she ever found out I told you this, but I can't be quiet. She's my best friend. And quite frankly, you're the first guy I've ever seen her show any spark with." She cleared her throat and glanced away again. "I just wanted you to know I think her divorce was harder on her than she lets on."

"So, in other words, don't hurt her."

She blushed and nodded. "Yeah."

"Noted." But he wouldn't promise. He couldn't.

He made his way back to Abby's truck and opened the driver's door. She rested her head on the back of the seat. As he climbed in, she turned to look at him. He held out the phone and she reached for it. "Thanks. But what about your SUV?"

"Earle is going to have it brought out to your place."

She slowly nodded, then winced. He started the truck and headed out of the parking lot. The only sounds for miles were their breathing and the rumble of the truck engine. He tapped his fingers against the steering wheel to the beat of the song he and Emily had written together.

He hit a pothole as he turned onto the country road leading to her ranch.

"Stop the truck."

He glanced at her. She clutched at her belly, and even in the dim light of the dashboard, he could see her face was turning three shades of green. "Hold on."

There was no room on the side of the road to pull off, so he stopped in the middle of the driving lane and hit the hazard lights.

She moaned again. "I'm gonna be sick."

As he unlatched his seatbelt, he swung open his door. She fumbled with the door handle on her side. He rushed around the truck and threw open her door, then reached over her to unclip her seatbelt. She let him help her out of the truck.

Before he was able to get out of the way, she heaved and spewed everything in her belly all over his jeans and thousand-dollar, genuine ostrich skin, custom-made boots.

When she was finished, she pushed her hair back and looked up at him, eyes huge with embarrassment. She wiped her mouth and whispered, "I-I'm sorry."

He glanced down at the mess and couldn't even be mad at her. "Remember that time when we went to the Founder's Day fair, and rode that carnival ride? What was it called?"

She closed her eyes. "The Whip-a-Whirl. I'd gorged myself on cotton candy and soda-pop right before I let you talk me into riding it."

Laughing, he helped her back into the truck. "And I paid for it when all that cotton candy and soda-pop ended up all over my lap."

She groaned and let out a choked chuckle, hiding her face in her hands. "You had to remind me. I was so nervous because you'd kissed me earlier that day back at the Double K. I hoped to impress you and instead ended up puking all over you."

Is that why you downed four beers in less than an hour? Do I make you nervous?

Yeah, right.

He leaned into the opening and snapped her seatbelt around her again. They were so close he could have kissed her if he wanted to--which he definitely wanted to, but not right now. His belly rolled, and he swallowed.

"You remember that first kiss, don't you, Seth?"

Oh, he remembered. He was fifteen and she was fourteen, and the memory of it easily gave him a hard-on for a long time afterward. Scared the hell out of him. But he'd never forgotten his first kiss. "I remember." He brushed her hair out of her face and smiled. "You were so shy."

"I couldn't believe you kissed me."

"Let's get you home."

After closing her door, he grabbed a clump of dried grass and used it to get the worst of the vomit off his jeans and boots, all while swallowing back his own. Thank God, he still had the new clothes he'd bought earlier today in the Escalade. If he had to, he'd run over to the Double K and shower and change before going back to Johanna's place.

He headed around the front of the rig when headlights damn near blinded him as they came to a stop in front of the truck on the wrong side of the road. The driver of the Tahoe opened the door, and the McAllister County Sheriff's Department logo flashed him.

He squared his shoulders and shifted his feet apart as Mike got out of the cruiser. He adjusted his gun belt like some Old West outlaw. "Seth? That's Abby's Silverado, isn't it? What's going on?"

Abby opened her door and stumbled out of the truck. She sidestepped her mess in the ditch and staggered to him. Why the hell didn't she just stay put?

"I'm taking Abby home."

A large box truck slowed as it passed by them. Mike waved and watched it as it headed down the road to the intersection. The driver had to be lost. There were only a handful of ranches between here and the end of the line at the Circle R.

Mike shifted his feet and the gun belt again as if uneasy. He looked Seth up and down then gazed at Abby. "You're drunk?"

She shrugged and grabbed Seth's arm to keep from tripping over her own feet. "Yep. You know me. No tolerance."

Mike narrowed his eyes into slits and moved a few steps closer. "You were out together?"

She stiffened and shook her head. "No. He was at Gatlin's, and I--"

"So what if we were?" Seth cut her off. "She doesn't answer to you anymore."

"Maybe not, but I don't want you near my daughter."

Jesus, help him. He wanted to knock Mike into next week every time he called Emily his daughter. "And you know I could prove publicly just how much of a sham that is."

He could, but he wouldn't.

Mike lost some of the constipated look as his eyes widened ever so slightly.

Looking down into Abby's upturned face, he said, "You haven't told him?"

"Told me what?"

He met Mike's dark gaze and shrugged. "It's simple. You and Abby let me get to know Emily and I won't sue you for custody. I think we all know a simple DNA test will prove which one of us is her father."

Mike's expression turned from one of surprise to fear in a millisecond. But soon, the constipated look was back worse than before. He bore down on him and got into his face. "You son-of-a-bitch. Do you know what that would do to her?"

Abby started shaking and her eyes got that glossy look to them. She was either going to puke again or cry. Seth didn't know if he could handle either reaction. He turned her around and headed for her side of the truck.

Her eyes pleaded with him as she peered up at him. He could only assume she didn't want him to knock Mike into next week.

He made his way around to the prick again, fisting his hands to fight the urge to grab him by the shirtfront. "Let's get something straight. I'm not going anywhere. At least not for a little while, and when I do leave, I'll be back. I don't really give a rat's ass how much you don't want me around Emily."

Mike glanced at the truck before turning toward his SUV. "Get Abby home. You both stink."

He sucked in a breath when a realization as bright as noon on a clear day hit him. He laughed and slapped his hand against his thigh. Mike faced him, and Seth said, "I'll be damned. Tammy Jo doesn't know Emily isn't yours. You never told her the truth that you only married Abby for her money."

Mike flicked his gaze toward Abby in the truck before he got so close to his face he smelled the stale coffee and something sweet and pepperminty on his breath. "I raised your bastard, Kendall." His voice was not much more than a growl. "And I'll do everything in my power to make sure she never learns the truth."

Seth stood there as Mike got into the cruiser and peeled out so fast the wheels protested with a squeal. The back tires missed running over his toes by mere inches. *What are you really afraid of, Mike? Hurting Emily, or your wife's wrath?*

He got into the truck and cranked the engine. Abby stared out the side window, but he knew from the way her shoulders trembled she was crying.

He wanted to ask her about Mike, but now wasn't the time. As much as he wanted to know the truth so he could use it as leverage over her and Mike, he wouldn't stoop low enough to take advantage of her at her most vulnerable.

He helped her out of the truck and up to the front of the single-story ranch house. From her unsteady hands, he took her key and opened her door. He got her inside to the kitchen and sat her in a chair at the big country table.

She groaned and buried her face in her hands. He rummaged around the kitchen cupboards until he found the fixings to brew a pot of strong coffee. Handing her a cup, he said, "Drink this. It'll make you feel better."

"I can't believe this." She looked up at him and took the cup between her shaky hands. "You probably think I'm some kind of drunk."

He snorted and sat at the table. "No. But I am wondering why you drank so much."

She avoided answering by sipping the coffee then winced. "I hate black coffee."

"It's better for your belly that way."

She took a few more sips, then set the cup on the table and sighed. "Why are you doing this, Seth?"

"Doing what?"

"Being nice to me."

He sucked in a breath and looked down at his hands. "A part of me wonders what would have happened if you'd have come with me that night."

She leaned over her arms and stared into the cup. "Don't."

He snagged her gaze and held it. "Did you love Mike?"

She tilted her head until her hair slid over her face, and her gaze slipped from his. "Yes."

A horn blew from the driveway, and he stood. "That's probably Earle. Will you be okay?"

Nodding, she sipped the black coffee again and grimaced. "Go. I'll be fine."

Without another word, he left the house. He thanked Earle for bringing his rig out and assured him Abby was okay. Then the man got into the truck that had followed him and the driver turned around.

He got in the Escalade. The stink from the vomited beer coating his jeans was really starting to make him sick. He would never make it to town. Without another look back, he turned around and headed toward the Double K.

He parked in front of the house and grabbed one of the clothes bags from the passenger seat. Johanna had given him an extra key last week when he came out to the ranch to go riding, but he'd never used it. Now, he opened the kitchen door and let himself in.

The real estate agent was to come by Monday to get the place on the market. According to him, the housing market might suck, but farms and ranches were still selling well. He expected the place to go quickly-- especially with Seth's name connected to the place.

He glanced around the country kitchen. He wasn't sure what he felt about strangers moving into the house his great-grandfather built for his bride. He might have despised his old man, but he had never hated where he'd come from.

No use dwelling on what he'd planned to do with the house. Flipping off the light, he headed for the stairs and climbed to the second floor to the hall bathroom. He showered and put on the new clothes he'd bought for the show he planned to do at the nursing home Wednesday. He cleaned up his boots as well as possible, then grabbed all the dirty laundry and put it in an empty plastic bag to throw away later.

As he headed out of the bathroom, he couldn't help but notice the master bedroom door stood open. Johanna had started going through John's personal things. Piles of clothes were stacked on the bed.

He stopped at his old bedroom door and shifted the bag from one hand to the other. What had the old man done with all of his old stuff? Had he tossed it all? He cracked the door to the room, turned on the overhead light, and stepped back in time.

A quilt his Grandma Harris had made for him still covered the twin bed. His baseball collection and a photograph of him and Mike fishing sat on the dresser. Another of Abby from tenth grade sat on the nightstand.

Swallowing down the lump of memories, he lifted his eyes to a framed, autographed t-shirt hanging on the wall above the bed. Although he'd once been the opening act for George Strait and considered the King of Country Music his friend, he would never forget the concert when he was sixteen and first met his greatest musical influence.

Or the way Abby had held his hand throughout the whole thing.

He turned to leave and staggered back. Over his old desk hung a collection of framed local newspaper clippings about his success, and programs from the concerts he'd done in several Texas and western Oklahoma cities. Had his dad gone to them?

A shadow box held a CD copy of his first album. He gaped at the collection. Why had Dad kept all this stuff?

His gaze touched the photographs he'd sent his father out of spite when he'd won the Horizon Award and Best Male Vocalist for the first time. Another frame held a picture of him accepting Entertainer of the Year for the first time. There was a picture of him receiving his first Grammy. The last one was of him standing barefoot on the beach with his St. Thomas house in the background. He wore Bermuda shorts, an open tropical shirt and a straw hat, and he held a beer in silent toast to the camera. On the bottom of the photo, he'd written *Merry Christmas from St. Thomas* as if it were a postcard.

He sank on the end of the bed and finally took a breath. Every CD he'd recorded was stacked on the desk. A shoebox held the few letters he'd written to his father. Mostly they were to brag about his success. Not once had he asked his dad how he was. He'd never expected the man to even read them, let alone keep them.

He felt numb at first, then confused. In all of his life, he'd never have thought his father would have a shrine dedicated to him. It touched something deep within him where that first flicker of grief had come to life. This time Seth didn't smother the spark, he let it smolder into an achy fire in his chest.

He left the house and got into his SUV. The letter, which he'd tossed onto the passenger seat three days ago, drew his attention, and he picked it up. He pondered his scrawled name on the front for a long moment before turning it over and opening it.

Dear Son,

If you are reading this, then I'm dead. I know it will be too late for much of what I'm about to say to even affect you, but I feel it has to be said. I suppose I'm also a coward because I'd rather tell you this after it no longer matters than tell you to your face and discover you actually do hate me.

Facing death has forced me to think about my life. I wish I'd done a lot of things differently. I'm dying with many regrets. Two of the most painful are what happened with your mother and how I treated you.

Regardless of what happened between your mother and me, I never stopped loving Suzie. Even when she betrayed me, I loved her. I still love her today. And I realize I should have let her follow her dreams.

I have no excuse for what happened between you and me except I was afraid you'd end up like your mother. It scared me to think you would turn to drugs and alcohol, especially if things got rough for you in the pursuit of your dream. I was wrong. You aren't like her at all.

I've never been much of a father to you. Go after what you want, son. Go after her with everything you have. I know about Abby, and I know about the secret she's kept. Ask her about it. Then the reason I didn't leave you the ranch will make sense. And I hope you do the right thing.

I was too stubborn to admit you had to live your own life, and you were too stubborn to see I was just too proud to admit I was scared. You've always been like me in this respect. Stubborn and proud. I'm too much of both to know when to say I'm wrong and when to say I'm sorry.

But I am, Seth. I'm sorrier than you'll ever know. I'm sorry for all the times I hit you, I'm sorry for the time I ran you off, and I'm sorry for all the mean words. None of this can be taken back, but I hope you know that, if I could, I would do so in a heartbeat.

I hope someday you can forgive me. I love you, Seth. I'm so damned proud of you.

Dad

He read the letter three times. His hands shook as he held the pages, and his vision blurred. He couldn't hold the wash of silent tears back. The mild pain in his chest was now a deep ache stealing his breath. He read the last couple of lines again, and a sob tore loose from the tightness in his chest.

He hadn't cried since he was nineteen, but back then it had been from the hurtful things his father had said and the disgust in his eyes as he'd run him off with a shotgun. Now, the tears formed from grief, regret and relief.

He'd made his father proud.

His father had loved him.

Looking up at the house in the moonlight, he knew exactly what he had to do.

"Oh, Dad, you're wrong again. It does matter to me. It will always matter to me." He pounded a fist on the top of the steering wheel and closed his eyes against the burning of bitter tears. Goodbye, Dad.

* * * *

Abby woke up to the sound of a banshee screaming in her ears. She groaned and flipped the pillow over her head. It didn't help. The terrible ringing didn't stop.

Ringing?

She jumped up and instantly wished she hadn't. The bright sunlight coming through the gingham curtains knifed through her retinas like a surgeon's laser. Squeezing her eyes closed, she fumbled for the telephone and blessedly silenced the banshee.

Holding her head with her free hand, she tried to swallow the cotton in her mouth, but it just stuck in her throat. "'Ello?"

"How you feeling this morning?"

She blinked, fell onto the bed and covered her head with the covers--phone and all. "Like I've been dragged twenty-five miles over rough ground. Then a whole herd of pregnant cows tap danced over me."

Seth chuckled and the sound attacked her ear with razor sharp teeth. "That good?"

She held the phone away from her offended ear. "Oh, laugh it up, cowboy."

"Hey, who ended up puking on whom--not once in her life but twice?"

"Dear God, are you never gonna let me live that down? I didn't ruin your boots, did I? They looked expensive."

"No, you didn't ruin my boots. But I retired the jeans."

Too, bad. You looked damned good in them.

He laughed again. Sweet mercy, she hadn't said the words aloud, had she? Feeling a bit claustrophobic under the blankets, she flipped them away and squeezed her eyes closed against the light.

"I'll assume you are still a bit inebriated."

I am. This time, she made sure she kept her lips closed. Taking a deep breath, she switched the phone to her other ear. "Thanks for getting me home last night."

"Don't mention it." There was a pause on the other end of the line, but she knew he had more to say. "Hey, I was hoping you and Emily would go riding with me this afternoon. Maybe have dinner at Grandpa's old hunting cabin."

At the mention of Emily, she sat straight up in bed and quickly regretted the sudden move when her head swirled and her stomach flopped over. "What time is it?"

"A little before ten. C'mon, Abby, you know it's foolish--"

"Damn, I need to pick up Emily from her friend's in less than..." She squinted at the bedside clock. "Ten minutes."

She got out of bed and groaned as the world tilted and spun. "Whoa."

Sitting on the bed, she waited until the room stopped circling her.

"Abby, you okay?"

"No. I swear on everything holy I'll never get drunk again."

"Why don't I pick Emily up and bring her home?"

She rubbed the back of her neck. "I should call Mike."

But she hated to do that. Mike would get Emily tomorrow for the next week. Besides, the last thing she wanted to admit to her ex, friend or not, was that she was too hung-over to take care of her daughter. Bad enough he'd seen her last night.

"Why are you being so stubborn about this? Are you trying to punish me or something?"

Was she? Maybe she was. "I'm afraid that she'll..."

"She'll what? Like me? Become my friend? Realize I'm her father?"

She held her aching head and closed her eyes. "Yes," she breathed out. "I'm afraid, if she finds out the truth, she'll want to go to Nashville with you."

"She wants to be a singer, doesn't she?" he finally asked after a long pause.

She didn't miss the husky quake in his voice. "She's wanted to be a singer like you since she was four years old."

"Abby, she's my daughter." He cleared his throat, but the heavy emotion weighed down his voice, making it even deeper than normal. "I only want to get to know her..."

His voice cracked, and with it, Abby's resolve. "Okay. You pick her up, and after you bring her home, we'll spend the day together."

"Thank you."

She gave him the address to Emily's friend and hung up.

She wasn't sure how long she sat there. Had she been wrong to let Mike talk her into hiding Emily's paternity? She'd been so sure then. Had been until she heard the pain in Seth's voice.

Mike asked her not reveal the truth to Emily, and for right now, she agreed the time wasn't right. Emily would never understand her reasons for not going with Seth and then marrying another man. Hell, she barely understood them herself.

She went to the closet and pulled a large shoebox from the top shelf. Slowly, she removed the lid and she stared at the crayon drawings, the duplicate photographs of the ones in her scrapbooks, and the copied DVDs. She'd told Mike when he left that he couldn't have the things in the box because she'd collected them for Emily.

Now, she allowed herself to admit the truth.

She'd kept this stuff for Seth.

Chapter 7

Seth pulled up to the curb in front of the nondescript home of Emily's friend. Across the street, live oaks and shrubs shrouded the elementary school. He glanced at his hat on the side seat, ran his hand through his hair, and then adjusted his sunglass. Maybe he'd be less recognizable without his hat and with the shades on.

He could hope.

As he got out of the SUV, he heard loud music coming from the back of the house. He followed the sound to the backyard. From a sound system, the Zack Brown Band finished singing about their toes in the sand, and the opening to his latest number one blared in his ears.

When Emily jumped off the lounge chair, he paused behind the shrub at the corner. She stood on the patio by the pool and broke into song. Her clear, strong voice crowded out his as she sang with him about drinking away a bad romance. Three other girls sat around in the shade of an overhang and laughed as Emily gyrated her hips to the fast beat of the beer-drinking song. She pretended her soda can was a microphone and threw her hand up as she hit the final line of the chorus. *"Havin' one helluva time drinkin' your memory away."*

Her audience laughed and clapped while Emily bowed low. "Thank you," she said, mimicking Elvis--of all people. "Thank you, very much."

He laughed and blew his cover. She and the three girls gaped as he rounded the bush. The girls squealed and Emily stood there with her mouth open.

"Not bad. Not bad at all. But I hope it's a long time before you really get the meaning of that song."

"Seth?"

"You know him?" One of the girls whipped her head around to stare at her.

"Yeah, he's friends with Mom and Dad." Emily smiled and shrugged. "Seth and I have been hanging out. He's really cool."

"No way!" Three high-pitched voices sang out.

He rubbed his goatee. "Your mom asked me to pick you up."

"Mom?" She narrowed her eyes. "You saw Mom this morning?"

"I talked to her on the phone. She wasn't feeling well and asked me to come get you." He took his Ray-Bans off and smiled at the other girls. "Ladies."

They were too shocked to do much but gawk between him and Emily.

"Okay." Emily set her can on the patio table then turned to her stunned friends and pointed at each girl in turn. "Seth, these are my BFFs. Lacy, Allie and Jasmine." She flourished her hand toward him. "BFFs, meet the one and only, great Seth Kendall."

Lacy somewhat recovered from being starstruck. "It's so nice to meet you, Mr. Kendall."

"It's great to meet you too."

Lacy's mother came out the side door and insisted he have a glass of iced tea. The girls were further stunned by the fact he and she had sat next to each other in sixth grade and had his aunt as their teacher. He signed autographs for the girls and his old classmate, then he and Emily left for the ranch.

* * * *

Abby had finished packing a picnic lunch for later at the cabin, when someone pounded on the back door. She wiped her hands on a dishtowel and opened the kitchen door.

Mike stood in the opening, his expression hard and his brown eyes dark under the brim of his hat. He shoved his hands into the pockets of his jeans. "We need to talk."

She swallowed and allowed him to enter. "What's going on?"

He took his hat off, tossed it on a hook by the door and faced her with a glare. "Is he still here?"

"Who?"

"Seth. He's always been your weakness." Mike walked around the kitchen before meeting her gaze again. "Are you sleeping with him?"

She'd been honest with Mike while they'd been married. He'd known she'd loved Seth in a way she hadn't been able to love him, but he'd loved Tammy Jo. And he hadn't always been honest with her. Abby hadn't known about his two-year affair with Tammy Jo until she'd asked him if he was having one.

He had no right to jealousy. And more importantly, he had no right to question her. She had the divorce decree to prove it.

Her head still ached a little, and she wasn't in a mood to deal with any of this--whatever this was. She crossed her arms and jutted her chin. "Even if I was sleeping with Seth Kendall, it wouldn't be any of your damned business."

"Maybe not, but what about our agreement concerning Emily?"

She dropped her arms. "What agreement?"

He strode toward her until he was in front of her. "Emily isn't to learn the truth. And the only way to keep it from her is to keep him away from her."

She sighed and turned toward the sink. As she stared out the window above it, she said, "I can't do that anymore. He deserves to get to know her."

He grabbed her by the shoulder and turned her around. His face and eyes filled with black fury. "No. Damn it. In the eyes of the law, I'm her father. I don't want her to have anything to do with him."

She straightened and squared her shoulders. "Why, Mike?"

"Seth walked out of here and hasn't been back once in fourteen years. If he'd wanted to be a father, he wouldn't have stayed away."

Mike wouldn't even let me see my daughter. I was a fool when I let him talk me out of being in her life after she was born. Seth's words echoed in her mind.

"What exactly did you say to him that day he came back after her birth?"

Mike shrugged and turned away. "How the hell am I supposed to remember?"

A cold lump formed in her belly. He was lying. "Did you tell Seth to stay away from here? I know you said something."

He faced her again and fisted his hands by his side. "Yes. If you want to know the truth. I told him he'd end up just like his parents. He didn't want Emily." His voice softened. "He never loved you, Abby. All that night was to him was sex, and he regretted that you got pregnant."

A piece of her shattered. She didn't want to believe him, even though she'd said those very same words. "Why did you marry me?"

He touched the back of his fingers to her cheek and smiled. "You and Seth were my best friends. I knew what your having an illegitimate child would do to your already shaky reputation. I couldn't let that happen to you."

She stepped away and busied herself with rearranging the fruit in the bowl on the counter. Oh, yes, her reputation--the daughter of a disgraced preacher and an Indian prostitute. It didn't matter her mother gave up that life when she met her father. She'd never fit into the idyllic community of McAllister. And Charles Crawford had never been allowed on the pulpit again because he'd fallen in love with a hooker instead of just saving her soul.

Maybe if her mother hadn't shown up five months pregnant on their wedding day, things might have been different.

But that wasn't the real reason Mike had married her. She had to know the truth--the real reason. Not his standard answer. "Mike..." She turned and leaned against the counter. "That isn't what I asked. You've told me this for years. What did you get out of marrying me? It's not like you were in love with me. You've always loved Tammy Jo."

He looked down at his hands and turned away from her. "Your money helped pay the back taxes and the mortgage on the Circle R."

She should have been surprised, but she wasn't. Maybe she'd always known. "You married me for my money?"

He faced her again and reached for her. Holding her by her upper arms, he gazed into her eyes. "You make it sound like you didn't get anything out of our marriage. I became the father of your baby. I learned to love her as my own. And I won't allow you or anyone else to take her away from me."

She laid her hand on the roughness of his cheek. He hadn't shaved that morning. "I've made such a mess of everything. I have to try to make things right. All Seth wants is to get to know her. I think that's best."

He backed away as if she'd slapped him. "What if she finds out we lied to her? How do you think that will affect her? My mother and father? My position as sheriff?"

"I can't predict how she'll react, but I do know we better talk to her soon. When Emily's eighteen, it'll be too late." Her voice shook and she wrapped her arms around her middle against the sudden chill.

"What the hell are you talking about?"

"Both Seth and John have trust funds for her. When she turns eighteen, she'll be one very rich young woman."

His face lost some of its deep tan. "Seth told his father?"

She shook her head. "John and Johanna figured it out on their own." She shivered again and tightened the hug around her middle. "Don't you think it's time we face the truth ourselves? Seth is Emily's father, and it's time they were allowed to have a relationship."

* * * *

As Seth drove up the driveway, Abby stood in the doorway of the barn. She'd already saddled her pinto mare and chosen a gelding for Seth from her other horses. She'd informed Judd, her foreman, she'd be going riding and wouldn't be back until later that afternoon.

Seth stopped his Escalade in front of the barn, and he and Emily got out.

Emily ran around the front of the SUV and literally bounced on her toes with excitement. "Mom! Is it true? Seth said we're going riding over on the Double K today."

Abby laid her hand on her shoulder and glanced at Seth. He took her breath away, standing silhouetted against the late morning sun. "Yep. It's true. Go change and I'll saddle your horse."

Emily beamed at her, then at him before running into the house.

He watched her before turning his bright smile on Abby. "Thank you for today."

She nodded and turned to go back inside the barn. "I've decided you should get to know her. It'll make things easier when she turns eighteen and learns the truth."

When he sucked in a breath, she looked over her shoulder at him. He stood behind her and she turned.

"What changed your mind?"

She looked past him toward the house to make sure Emily had gone inside, then met his gaze. "A lot of little things, I guess. Your persistence. The fact you didn't drive away the day after the funeral. The trust funds. The story about you buying her a big teddy bear and still having it. I think she needs to get to know you. And I need to get to know you again." She shrugged and cleared her throat, but the lump wouldn't budge. "When the time comes, the three of us--you, me and Mike--will tell her the truth."

He stepped toward her. The clean, masculine scent of his musky cologne and something entirely Seth enveloped her. His warmth surrounded her. She trembled from the heat in his deep mossy green eyes.

His breaths came faster, making that wonderful chest rise and fall, and she had to touch him. She laid her hand on the great expanse of toned muscle and curled her fingers in the soft cotton of his shirt. He wrapped his arms around her waist and pressed her against the stall door. The horse's snort seemed to come to her ears from a great distance as he tilted his head toward hers. His breath warmed her face as electricity coursed between them. Then he brushed his lips against hers.

She fisted her free hand into the hair at his nape, pulling him closer, as he deepened the kiss. His tongue was sweet and hot, a velvety reminder of the passion she'd only ever felt in his touch. He rubbed down her sides to her behind and lifted her up against him. She wrapped her legs around his thighs, pulling him closer.

She moaned when the hard length of his arousal pressed against her center. She chased his tongue, and as he tried to retreat, she sucked on it, eliciting a lusty groan from deep in his chest. She let her other hand roam over his shoulders, up into his hair, pushing off his hat.

"Momma?"

They both froze at the softly spoken word. When she looked past his shoulder toward the door, Emily stood there peering at them with her mouth hanging slightly open, eyes wide.

Abby immediately untangled herself from him and tried to shove him away. "Seth is helping me with the horses."

Seth and Emily gawked at her with nearly identical expressions of bemusement, and she shoved at him harder. He let her down, but positioned himself behind her and held her close. She glanced questioningly at him. He raised an eyebrow, grinned, and leaned in to whisper in her ear, "I don't think you want me to move right now." She closed her eyes and trembled at the low rumble of his voice. "I'm hard as a rock."

"Oh. Don't move," she whispered and made sure she was directly in front of him. Swallowing hard, she turned to face her daughter, feeling very much like a teenager caught by a parent. Who would have thought the same embarrassment could be inspired with the reversed situation?

Seth chuckled, leaned over to pick his hat off the floor, and slapped it on his thigh before putting it on his head.

As if she'd figured something out that had stumped her for a long time, Emily tapped her forehead and said, "Crap, I always knew I was doing something wrong when I saddle my horse. Now I know. I gotta get myself a cute guy and swap spit and play tonsil hockey with him to get the job done."

She and Seth said at the same time, "I don't think so."

As soon as the words had left their mouths, Abby turned to meet his startled expression. Seth shrugged and rubbed his goatee. "She's too young to even be considering if a guy is...uh...well, you know."

"Yeah, I do know." She met Emily's intense gaze. What was she thinking? Was Emily happy about her kissing Seth? Or was she resentful because he wasn't Mike? "What took you so long to change?"

Emily laughed and rolled her eyes. "Well, I'm glad I didn't come out sooner. Trevor Marshall called." She slyly smiled and looked down as she clasped her hands together. "He invited me to the movies tonight, but I told him I'd have to pass it by you first."

"We'll discuss it later."

"Momma, you never let me--"

"Who's Trevor?" The edge on Seth's voice zapped through her. Emily must have been taken aback too, judging by the startled expression on her face.

Abby glanced over her shoulder to find his usually playful mouth compressed into a thin line and his jaw tight.

Was it just her fogged mind or had she just seen a flash of him as a father? For the first time, she pictured him as Emily's father. With all the wild oats he'd sown, no doubt, he'd be over-protective of his daughter.

Mike had been as protective of Emily as any other father was of his daughter, but he was too concerned these days with his new wife and unborn son to be worried about the boys who wanted to date Emily. Wannabe cowboys with vehicles and ideas that could land them both in trouble.

Emily bristled, putting her hands on her hips and jutting her chin. "He's one of my best friends and lives near Dad. He let me go with Trevor the last time I stayed with him and the witch."

"How old is this guy?"

She glared at Seth, her tone turning caustic. "Sixteen. But we really are just friends. So, Seth, what are your intentions with my mother, since my friends don't go around lip-locking with me?"

Abby was too surprised by Emily's question to even reprimand her for rudeness.

If her question affected him, he didn't show it. He simply shrugged and tightened his hold on her waist where he still held her against him. She gazed up at him, and he smiled a sexy lopsided grin. "I actually hoped your momma would go out with me and maybe help me decide what to do with the house on the Double K."

"You're moving onto the Double K?" Emily asked the question Abby was too stunned to ask.

"It would seem so," he answered Emily, but never looked away from Abby.

"You're buying the Double K?" She shivered, and her voice shook.

"Yeah. I think that's best, don't you?"

She nodded and turned toward him. Her heart filled to overflowing. The two deep seas of his eyes swept her away. She was drowning in them, but she didn't want to be saved. "What about this date?"

"Well, I figured we could go to the movies. Sit a few rows behind Emily and her friend."

Emily groaned, and Abby laid her head on his shoulder and laughed. He pressed up close. She relaxed against him and felt his lingering passion. She was too tired of being alone and pretending her life was perfect. She was too tired of fighting what she felt for him. And in giving up the fight, she lost another chunk of her heart to him.

"I think that's a perfect date," she whispered.

The passion of his kiss drowned out Emily's fading, "Holy crap!"

* * * *

Seth reined in his horse in front of the old single-room hunting cabin his grandfather Kendall built in a grove of ponderosa pines and hackberry trees near a stream that cut across the ranch. He glanced over his shoulder as Abby and Emily halted their mounts.

Emily looked around and pushed her hat back. "Wow. I never knew this place was even here. What a great cabin. Wish I'd found it before now."

He glanced at Abby as he dismounted his borrowed horse. "Did you explore the Double K a lot?"

"Oh, yeah. I love this place. Sometimes your dad would ride with me," Emily explained as she dismounted. She slipped the bridle from her mare's head.

"Your father let her have free range of the ranch." Abby slid out of her saddle, and his heart raced with the sight of her ass moving in the worn jeans. The blood rushing south fogged his brain so much he nearly missed what she'd said.

Emily undid the cinch and hefted the saddle off the sorrel's back. She set the saddle on the weathered banister of the porch covering the front of the cabin. "I like the Double K more than the Circle R."

"Really?"

"Yeah. The K isn't as flat as the R. Besides, Dad never liked me roaming over the R." Emily headed for the door.

"You'll need this."

She turned and easily caught the key ring he tossed to her, unlocked the door and entered the dark interior. "Awesome!"

He met Abby's amused dark eyes when she looked over at him. A light breeze ruffled strands of hair around her face under the brim of a straw cowboy hat. The rest of that gloriously thick mane hung over her shoulder in a loose braid.

He pulled her to him and brushed her mouth with his. Hell, he wanted to do more than that, but considering their teenage daughter was just inside, he refrained from sticking his tongue down her throat this time. When he pulled back, she slowly opened her eyes.

"Eww..." He looked over at the porch where Emily stood in the doorway with her hands on her hips. "Okay, I don't mind you two dating or whatever, but please try to not do the smooching thing when I'm around. Geez. It's bad enough I have to watch Dad and TJ make puppy dog eyes at each other and listen to them call each other cupcake and sweetpea. It's absolutely nauseating."

He chuckled and glanced at Abby, touched her face and thrilled when she shivered. "Okay, sunshine, you have a deal. I won't kiss your mother except behind closed doors."

"I don't want to hear about you and her having sex, either!" Emily scrunched up her face and headed inside again.

"Wait, that's not what..." He glanced at Abby, who shook her head and laughed. He pointed toward the cabin. "You know that's not what I meant, right?"

"Oh, you dug that grave all on your own, cowboy." Abby moved away and removed the bit from her pinto. "She's taking to you being around rather well."

He sucked in a breath heavy with the scent of horse, pine, wild flowers, and Abby. Things were too good to be real.

Shaking himself into action, he tended to his mount. "I'm glad, because I don't intend to go anywhere for a little while."

She set her saddle beside Emily's on the banister. "Don't you have to go back to Nashville soon?"

He paused in unbuckling the cinch "Yeah, but I can delay it for a couple more weeks until the paperwork for the ranch is finished."

She picked up the saddlebag containing their lunch and faced him. "What made you decide to buy the ranch?"

Emily reappeared in the doorway and placed the back of her hand dramatically over her forehead. "Are we ever gonna eat? I'm starving. Fading away into oblivion while you two play kissy face."

He shook his head and took the bag from Abby. "We'll talk while we eat." With his free hand on the small of her back, he led her across the porch. At the door, he tugged one of Emily's pigtails. "Well, we can't have that, now can we, sunshine?"

* * * *

"Will you be at the show Wednesday?" Seth stood at the door of his Escalade after dropping Abby and Emily home following the movie.

The warm breeze caught Abby's hair, sending strands of it into her face. He fought the urge to run his fingers through it. She smoothed the wayward hair back in place. "I'll be working, so I'll be there. I hear Clint's band is playing with you, too."

"I had planned on doing an acoustic show, but after playing with those guys, I thought I'd ask them to see who'd be willing to play with me again."

"It's really nice of you to put on a show."

He rubbed the beard at his chin. It needed trimming. "Thanks. I actually prefer the intimacy of a show like this or the impromptu one at Gatlin's. Singing before a stadium full of people is so much more stressful."

She pushed her hands into the back pockets of her jeans. "I can only imagine. I'd hate getting up in front of a crowd the size of the one at Gatlin's."

"Still shy, huh?"

She shrugged and looked down. "I guess. I never was like you." She met his gaze again. The light from the porch was dim. He could barely make out her bemused expression. "But then that's one of the things I always admired about you."

He leaned against the driver's door of the SUV. "I always loved your spirit. You never let anyone trample you into the dust."

Although the air was far from cold, she shivered and crossed her arms.

He pulled his keys from his pockets. "Thanks for today."

"You're welcome. Emily had a blast."

Tossing the keys from one hand to the other, he glanced at the house. "I did too. She's a special little girl."

"She's not so little anymore."

The twist to his heart brought him up short. "No, she isn't. I wish I'd known her before now."

Abby shifted her feet and looked down at the ground. Was she ashamed of the years she and Mike had stolen from him?

"Seth, try to be patient." She rested her hands on his chest and moved in close. He wrapped his arms around her, and she smiled. "I'm working most of this coming week, but I'd like to see you again."

"I'd like that too." He was on his way to Brokenheartsville, but Abby had always been his weakness. Besides, getting close to her guaranteed he'd be able to get closer to Emily.

"Emily is with Mike this week, but would you like to have dinner here Saturday night?"

He stiffened and moved away from her. "I hoped Emily and I could have some time together."

"We've been over this. You'll be moving onto the Double K soon. But I think it would be best for you and Emily to form a relationship slowly."

He faced her and unlocked his jaw enough to grind out his words. "I know. But I sure as hell don't have to like it."

She sighed loud enough for him to hear it. "What happened that night you came here to see us?"

He rolled his shoulders, trying to release the sudden tension. It didn't work. "You weren't here. Mike said you were visiting your dad in the hospital. I wanted to see Emily. I just wanted to see her." He looked into the night heavy with late August heat and the pain of a regret-filled past. "He refused by telling me she was asleep and that I had no right since I hadn't been man enough to stick around to begin with."

She touched him on his arm, and he met her gaze. "He told you you couldn't be a good father because of your parents, didn't he?"

"I'll never forgive myself for believing him."

She wrapped her arms around his waist and laid her head on his shoulder. She was a perfect fit. "I'm sorry, Seth. I should have..." She pulled back and met his gaze. "I have something to give you. I'll be right back."

She hurried away and through the kitchen door. Did they have a future? Was he a fool for even considering having a relationship with her? She continued to lie to Emily and play into Mike's game. Whatever Mike was hiding, he intended to discover and expose.

Abby returned carrying a boot box. She held it out to him and smiled. "Here. This is for you."

He took the box and furrowed his brows. "What is it?"

She shrugged and clasped her hands together. "You'll see when you get back to your aunt's. I want you to have it. I know it won't replace the missing years, but..." She shrugged again and sniffed. "You'll see. Well, I'd better get inside."

"Tell you what. How about I take you out Saturday night instead of you cooking?" Shifting the box under one arm, he pulled her to him with his free hand.

She wrapped her arms around his neck. "Okay. I hate to cook anyway."

He chuckled, but quickly let desire take over as he kissed her. When he finally broke away, he whispered, "Goodnight, Abigail."

She opened her eyes and smiled. "Goodnight."

* * * *

Seth sat on his bed and opened the lid of the box Abby had given to him. He gasped when he saw what lay inside. Picking up the first photograph, his heart constricted. Abby stood on the porch of her house, wearing a simple pink sundress and showing off her rounded belly. He flipped the picture over. It was dated March 20--three days before Emily was born.

He slowly took out another photo. His breath caught and stuck in his throat. Abby lay on a hospital bed holding a crying, red-faced baby wrapped in a pink blanket. He ignored the image of a smiling Mike leaning in to kiss Abby on the forehead. He focused on his baby and let out the captured breath.

He lost all track of time as he studied each photograph and piece of childish artwork. It was well past two AM when he reached for his laptop to watch the DVDs. Emily's first Christmas, her birthdays, the first time she sang before an audience--her childhood captured in fuzzy video for prosperity.

Mike's hushed voice narrated the clip. "Emily is to take the stage next, singing *Twinkle, Twinkle, Little Star*."

He watched as five-year-old Emily took the stage of the McAllister Elementary School. She smiled big and shifted her feet as she sang the grade-school classic in a clear, nearly pitch perfect, little girl voice.

By the time he watched her last softball game captured on film, he had tears in his eyes and a heavy sharp pain in his chest. And he'd come to one very important decision.

Just getting to know Emily wasn't enough.

He would do anything to be her father, including seducing Abby to get what he wanted.

"I've missed out on enough of your life, sunshine. I'm not missing out on any more."

Chapter 8

"So, Abby." Jenny Lynn stirred cream into her coffee. "Are you ever gonna spill?"

Abby swallowed the bite of steak fajita and followed it with a sip of water. She ignored the speculative stares of her friends across the table from her. After Seth's concert at the nursing home, she and Jenny Lynn were taking Darlene out to dinner before she had to get back to Amarillo and her dying husband.

She set her glass on the table. "Spill what? My water?"

"You're a comedian. You know very well what." Darlene laid her napkin on the table beside her plate. "You were pretty darned cozy today with a certain hunk we all know and love."

"I still can't believe you didn't tell us you were actually friends with Seth Kendall," Jenny Lynn lamented.

"Friends?" Darlene snapped her head around to look at the younger woman. "I'd call it dating, if you ask me." She sat back with smug amusement twisting her lips and brightening her ruddy face. "I hear from a very trustworthy birdie he's arranged for a private table for two at the Lakeside Grille. Sounds like a date to me."

Jenny Lynn turned her wide eyes to Abby. "Dating? You're freakin' dating superstar Seth Kendall?"

She glanced around at the other tables in the crowded diner. "Shh! Keep your voice down. I might be dating Seth. But right now, we're still getting to know each other again. He's a lot different than he was fifteen years ago."

"I'd say so." Jenny's grin got bigger as she leaned back in her seat. "He's undoubtedly sexier. It's high time you start going out again. Mike had no problem moving on after you two entered Splitsville."

She couldn't argue with the truth. Seth had always been good-looking, but now he was all grown up. She wanted him, but she couldn't lose herself in him.

She was about to change the subject when Darlene said, "I agree with Jenny Lynn. You need to start living again."

"And who better to do it with." Jenny Lynn sipped her coffee. "So, what's he like?

She picked at the peppers on her plate with her fork. "He's fun, sometimes a little too full of himself, but I've always had a good time with Seth."

"Damn, girl, I wasn't asking about that."

She looked up, puzzled. Then it dawned on her. "You think I'm sleeping with him?"

"Hell, I would be."

"Well, I'm not you."

"Girls, let's remember we're in a public place," Darlene, who was older than Abby by more than ten years, chided in a motherly tone. Then the mother hen turned her attention on Jenny Lynn. "By the way, what's up with you and Wayne Cover? I thought you dumped him. But you were hanging all over him today after the concert."

Jenny shrugged and stirred her coffee again. Her turn to play coy. "We've decided to give it another try."

Abby, glad the focus was off her, smiled and sipped her water as the other women discussed the drummer's attributes.

She considered her date with Seth on Saturday. She'd originally invited him to her home. What had she expected to happen after she'd serve him dinner? She set her water down. Damn, was she that desperate? She may as well serve herself up on a platter with a bow around her neck.

Seth wanted her. He couldn't hide that fact, not after the kiss in the barn, or the many following it. But was she really ready to give herself to him?

She wasn't sure she liked the answer anymore. Her heart and its lusty wants were winning the battle with her fleeting pragmatism and caution.

"Okay, enough about me." Jenny Lynn pointed her spoon at her and speared her with a narrowed look. "You need to loosen up. Seth Kendall is sexy, rich, and obviously into you if he's wining and dining you. So, hell, use him while you can! Then you can fill us lesser mortals in on what we're missing." She took a bite of chili.

Darlene pushed her half-eaten meal away and leaned over her folded arms. "Jen's right--well, at least about this--you need a man in your life. I really don't need to hear details of what you do with him. But honestly, I think he'd be a good influence on Emily."

Her heart slammed into her ribs, and her blood froze in her veins. "What's that supposed to mean?"

Darlene shrugged and sipped her cola. "Just that we all know she wants to be a singer. I'm sure Seth has contacts and knows people who could make her dreams happen."

Her heart shifted into place and tingling replaced the numbness in her fingers and toes. "Mike doesn't want her to be a singer."

"Who the hell cares what that asshole wants?" Jenny Lynn folded her arms over her chest. "He left you, Abby. You painted a pretty convincing picture, but I know what really happened. He cheated on you and left you for Tammy Jo McAllister." She shifted forward and took her clammy hand. "I've seen the sparks. I know you're attracted to Seth, and he couldn't stop undressing you the other night at Gatlin's. I say go for it. See what happens. You deserve to be happy."

"You know I agree." Abby lifted her glass of water and took a drink. "Now, let's drop it, okay?"

They finished their meal, and after she hugged Darlene and Jenny Lynn, she headed into the ladies room and ran right into Glenda Marshall.

"I'm sorry," Abby murmured as she stepped back.

The mayor's wife wrinkled her nose and looked down at her suit as if Abby had soiled it from the light contact. "I've been meaning to call you."

"Oh?" Nothing good could come out of that phone call.

Glenda continued to look down her pudgy nose at her. Quite a challenge, since Glenda was easily three inches shorter than her. "Yes. I wanted to discuss your daughter chasing my son."

Emily chasing Trevor? She knew for a fact it was the other way around, especially after seeing the two together the other night at the movies. She stepped farther into the restroom. Her bladder was about to burst. "Emily and Trevor are just friends."

"Is that so? Wasn't that what you and Mike Ritter were? Just friends when you tricked him into marrying you by getting pregnant? And now that he finally cut you loose, you keep hanging on. Like some cancerous sore. But then, isn't that true for all of your people?"

She took a deep breath. *Your people.* She'd heard it all over the years. About the life of leisure on the reservations. About Indians getting rich on casinos. About their laziness and living off welfare.

A life her mother ran away from when she was seventeen, only to find out she had no skills and no job. The only thing she had was her body, and she'd used what she had to keep from starving on the streets.

Glenda's high heels clicked on the tile as she stepped in close behind her. "I won't have my son ruin his life by associating with your daughter. Like mother, like daughter. Your mother was a whore who lured a man of God in with her debauchery. You destroyed Mike's life. I won't allow your daughter to trap Trevor in the same snare."

She closed her eyes as Glenda's heels disappeared out the door.

When would she stop being punished for her parents' sins?

* * * *

Abby paced the living room floor with one recurring thought circling in her brain: *I have to be crazy.*

The chiming doorbell startled her.

Damn. She was used to working under pressure and stress, but the thought of going out with Seth made her as skittish as a mouse in a room full of hungry cats.

She sucked in a lungful of air and opened the door. When Seth's hot gaze slowly moved over her, she looked down to make sure her sundress was not burned to ash.

She swallowed and moved away from the door. "Hi."

"Good evening, Abigail." He smiled and held out a large bouquet of deep red roses. "These are for you. I remembered how you'd come over to the Double K and tend Grandma's old rose bushes just to pick the flowers."

"H--how did you remember that?" Was that breathy voice really hers?

"I remember lots of things," he said in that low, velvet voice for which he was famous. It made tingles go up her spine.

"Thank you." With trembling hands, she took the roses and breathed in their sweet fragrance. "They're beautiful."

Mike had never given her roses. Not like this.

She swallowed the lump in her throat and gripped the stems with both of her sweaty hands. "I'd better get these in some water. Come in."

His boots sounded hollow against the flooring as he followed her into the kitchen. The heat of his gaze warmed her while she busied herself with filling a vase, cutting the stems and arranging the blooms.

When she couldn't avoid facing him any longer, she turned and set the vase in the middle of the table. He'd leaned against the edge of the counter, crossed his booted ankles and folded his arms over his wide chest to watch her, completely at ease in his own skin.

He wore a black bolo tie held with a silver and turquoise clasp at the neck of his white western shirt. She looked over his shirt to the big, silver belt buckle low on his waist, but before she could study that area of his anatomy too much, she let her gaze drift down. The black jeans fit his long legs like a second skin.

"I see you got another pair of black jeans."

"Hopefully, I won't have to retire these as quickly as the last pair."

She felt her face get hot. How romantic. Reminding him about her puking all over him.

"You look good," he said.

"Thanks. You do too. I recognize the tie clasp." She cleared the sudden hoarseness from her throat. "It's from Johnson's Western in town. I bought the same one for Dad--I mean Frank--last year for Christmas."

"I found it the other day and liked it." He pushed away from the counter.

"The tie suits you." She dragged her gaze from him and sniffed the roses again. "These really are lovely. But you shouldn't have."

"You always were so girly, but pretended to be a tomboy just to fit in with Mike and me. I think sometimes he forgot that you were a girl." He drawled his words and pulled her in like a hapless fish on a line. "But I never did."

"No, you didn't."

He twisted his black cowboy hat in his hands then set the Stetson on his head. "Well, our reservation for the Lakeside is at seven-thirty. If you're ready, we'd better go."

His lips curled in one of his devilish smiles. She glanced at the strong, big hand he held out to her. They locked gazes as his fingers closed around hers. The comfort she found in his warm grasp washed over her, leaving her soul raw with the loneliness of the past several years.

* * * *

Twenty minutes later, the hostess whisked Seth and Abby through the dining room of the Lakeside Grille. A single, linen-draped table waited for them on a private covered terrace, overlooking the attractive manmade lake.

He held a chair out for her, and her light, flowery scent enticed without overpowering his senses. The pale yellow sundress hugged her curves and exposed her tanned back and shoulders. He helped scoot in her chair after she sat down. Her gaze touched his and heated him through until she shifted away, breaking the connection.

He sat across from her.

She avoided meeting his eyes again and fiddled with the cloth napkin folded into some fancy shape. She refolded the linen into a simple square then cleared her throat and looked up at him.

"Nervous?" he asked.

"Of course not." She smiled, but she didn't fool him. Abby was as restless as a penned up wild mustang. "I've never eaten here. But I've heard they have a fantastic menu. You're gonna spoil me."

"You deserve to be spoiled." He reached for the leather-bound menu, but didn't look at it. "I wanted to thank you for the box of Emily's stuff."

She pulled her hair over one shoulder. "You're welcome. I know it won't make the years suddenly reappear, but I hoped you'd see how happy she's been."

"She reminded me a lot of you, but more outgoing." He didn't want to dwell on what he'd missed.

She leaned back in her chair. "I never thought she was like me at all. She always reminded me of you."

He concentrated on not fisting his hand where it lay against his thigh. "When are we going to tell her the truth?"

"Seth, not now. Let's enjoy tonight, okay?"

He'd let her have tonight. But he refused to be leashed forever. "All right."

When the nervous waitress arrived, he playfully flirted with the young woman for a few minutes before ordering a bottle of champagne.

Abby smiled, but it never really reached her eyes. They were wary, as if she knew he wouldn't be appeased for much longer. She looked at the menu. "I think I'll try the shrimp scampi. I've heard great things about it."

"I wish I could still eat shrimp."

The yellow in her dress and the setting sun brought out the amber flecks hidden within her dark eyes. He tried to ignore the sudden tightening in his low belly without much luck.

The server returned, poured them each a glass of champagne and took their orders.

When the woman moved away, Abby raised a brow. "Champagne?"

He lifted his glass. "I thought we'd celebrate."

She smiled brightly and lifted her glass. "What are we celebrating?"

"Emily."

"To Emily." Her eyes glistened as she touched her glass to his then took a sip. "Okay, why the heck can't you eat shrimp? You loved it as a kid."

He set his glass on the table. "Unfortunately, the last time I ate it, I almost died."

"You almost died?" Her eyes widened and her kissable lips rounded. "Oh, no, have you become allergic to shrimp?"

He closed his hand around hers and rubbed his thumb over the soft skin. Her slight shiver had nothing to do with the sudden breeze. He definitely liked where the night was going. "About three years ago, I was at a Grammy party and had an allergic reaction after eating some shrimp. Good thing Amanda knew what was going on and got me to the hospital as quickly as she did. I ended up with anaphylaxis."

"That's scary." She took another sip of champagne and set the glass down. "I seem to remember hearing about you being rushed to the hospital on the radio." A frown puckered her brow, and she pulled her hand out of his. "Amanda? As in Amanda Lang?"

Damn, why had he mentioned the only woman whom he'd ever labeled as a girlfriend? "Yes, Amanda Lang. It's no secret we've been dating off and on for years."

"I know all about your dating her." She tidied the already straight silverware. "I'm surprised you never married her."

"And we would've ended up on that very long list of celebrities with really short marriages." He sighed and leaned over the table. "I never loved her and she never loved me."

Her eyes narrowed and her cheeks blossomed in a dark pink. "Oh, that's right, you're just friends--with benefits."

He straightened and fought the urge to grit his teeth. "Yes, Amanda and I have been friends since we competed on *America's Rising Star*. But our relationship didn't turn into something more than platonic until after you were married and your husband made it quite clear I wasn't wanted around here."

The color drained from her face. "I'm sorry. I didn't mean to sound so..."

"Jealous?" He relaxed and grinned as he reached across the table and took her hand. "I guess I should take that as a good sign. But I promise you, Amanda and I haven't been more to each other than friends--of the platonic kind and without any benefits--for over a year."

When he rubbed the soft place over the pulse of her wrist, the heat flashing in her eyes burned him clear to his bones.

* * * *

They finished their meals and shared decadent chocolate cake and rich coffee. She licked the icing off her fork and smiled. "That was truly better than..."

Seth raised a brow and set his cup on its saucer. "If you say sex, you've been missing out. The cake was good, but not that good."

Her face flamed hot, and she averted her eyes, but she couldn't deny what he said, so she laughed, which was better than climbing under the table.

She looked up when he reached across the table and rubbed his thumb along her cheek to her chin. "You are still the most beautiful woman in the world when you blush." His husky voice and warm touch caused a shiver to quake through her. "Dance with me."

She looked around. They were alone on the terrace. Soft music was piped through a sound system. Chinese lanterns lit the stone floor with multicolored lights. The sun had long ago gone down, and the stars reflected off the McAllister Reservoir below the bluff.

"Okay." When her eyes met his again, she knew exactly how this night would end. His eyes darkened with wanton lust.

He led her to the open floor and pulled her to him. She gave in to the feeling of his hands on her waist, burning though her thin dress, and her touch relaxed on his shoulders. She melted right into him.

He surrounded her. His hot breath in her hair where he rested his cheek against her temple and the warmth of his body against hers and the way he moved against her as they swayed to the music fanned the fire in her veins. She buried her nose in his neck and breathed in his heady, male scent. She trembled with an all-consuming need like nothing she'd ever felt.

She couldn't catch her breath. The song wound to its end while her heart galloped away. As she moved against Seth's hips, the evidence of his desire pressed against her lower belly. She'd never felt like this for Mike. And he'd never lusted for her.

As Seth moved against her again, all thoughts of Mike flew from her mind. She pulled away to meet his eyes ablaze with the same hot lust that had filled them on that magical night so long ago. She responded with an answering ache deep in the pit of her soul. Even after all these years, she wanted him, and like all those years ago, she would risk everything to have him.

"I think you'd better take me home."

"Yeah, I think that would be best," he said in a sexy drawl. A shudder quaked through her, and the last of her resistance crumbled. "Or I'm liable to do something that will definitely cause a whole heap of gossip."

* * * *

Abby didn't remember much of the drive home. Like a man possessed, Seth pulled into her drive and skidded to a stop on the loose gravel of the driveway.

He unfastened his seatbelt and leaned over at the same time she knelt in the leather seat facing him. Her arms went around his neck. His went around her waist and pulled her as close as the center console would allow.

Their lips clashed together, and he slid his hungry tongue into her mouth. She tasted the spicy passion sizzling between them, tangled her fingers into the strands of his hair, pulling him even closer. One of his hands slid up her side to cover her breast; the other slipped under her skirt and stroked the skin of her thigh, then slipped under the edge of her panties. When he stroked her, she shivered at the sensation of his rough hand so intimately touching her.

"Damn, you're so wet." He moaned as she sucked on his lower lip and nibbled on the captured flesh.

"Don't stop." She shivered again and her breathing went ragged. She was too close to the edge to not fall over it. When he slipped a finger inside her, it was too much. She clung to him as the shudders of her orgasm raked over her.

When she finally opened her eyes to meet his, he groaned as he pulled his hand away. His eyes were dark in the fickle light of the moon and porch shining through the windshield, but they burned with need.

"Let's go inside," she whispered against his lips.

He rushed around the SUV and yanked the door open. She went into his arms, wrapping her legs around his waist and her arms around his neck. He stopped and his breath hissed out of him, breaking the kiss.

"What's wrong?"

He untangled her legs from around his waist and shifted her into a bridal carry. "Trust me this way is safer. Or I'll strip you right here."

"At this point I don't care," she murmured and pulled his mouth back to hers. "I want you inside me."

He carried her to the front door. She fumbled with her key, while he suckled the soft skin behind her ear, making it damned hard to concentrate. When she finally got the door open, they didn't bother with the light; he went straight through the house to the master bedroom.

He set her on her feet and buried his fingers in her hair as he kissed her. She pulled his shirt out of his jeans and yanked open the pearl snaps. His chest quivered under her touch. He broke the kiss as she explored the hard muscle and contrasting textures of the curls and smooth skin.

She undid the clasp and tie, then he shucked the shirt. She bit her bottom lip as the dim moonlight from the windows limned his wide chest and muscular shoulders. She ached for him and couldn't wait much longer. As she reached for his belt, he reached around her and unzipped the dress.

He took possession of her mouth, his tongue plunging deep, imitating what they both wanted. Before his jeans slipped down his toned legs, he pulled a condom from his back pocket and placed it on the bedside table. He pushed the dress from her shoulders and it fell to the floor, followed by her bra and panties, then he lifted her against him again and laid her on the bed.

Moaning his name deep in her throat, she arched against him as he brushed his thumb over a puckered nipple. She reached between them and found his heavy erection. He broke the kiss with a hiss and caught her hands.

"You've got to slow down, baby." He pulled her arms over her head.

"I don't want slow." She arched her body into him again. "I want you inside now."

He growled and nuzzled her neck. "Jesus, I think you're gonna kill me."

"No, you're killing me." Was that breathy voice hers?

He shuddered then pulled back. "How can I want you this much?" he asked in a gravelly rumble that stilled her heart. "How did I survive without having you before now?"

For a long moment, she searched his gaze. What did he mean by that? "I swore this wouldn't happen. But I want you so much I can't breathe."

Trailing openmouthed kisses down her throat, he stopped to nibble on the skin over her racing pulse. His facial hair tickled her oversensitive skin as he placed soft kisses over her breasts and suckled on the hard points of her nipples.

"Seth, please."

He took the condom and quickly sheathed himself. Her heart pounded so fast and hard against her ribs she feared it would crash out of her chest. He was so big and it had been so long since she'd had sex. She hoped she could take him.

When he lay over her, he captured her lips with his. Legs wound around his hips, and arms clasped his shoulders, she held on to him, afraid to let go.

When his erection touched her, he closed his eyes and groaned deep in his chest. She moved against him, and he entered in a single thrust.

"Oh, God, Abby...you feel so good." His head went back; his jaw clenched taut. His shoulders and chest tensed. He was so beautiful, her soul wept.

"Seth."

He met her gaze with one heavy with desire as he moved over her and within her, finding the perfect rhythm.

Her nails bit into his shoulders as she urged him to move faster. Her body pulsed around him, taking him deeper. He consumed her, and she wanted to consume him. He dove into her over and over again, rushing them both to completion.

He gripped her hips, lifted her, angling her pelvis. She cried out at the jolt of pleasure flowing through her. A rattling groan came from his chest as she tightened around him, drawing him deep into her. His biceps bulged, and his face contorted with strained control.

Had she ever felt like this?

She screamed when the orgasm hit. Wave after wave of ecstasy washed over her heated flesh, and light burst behind her eyes. Calling out his name, she held on to him and rode out the storm.

He plunged into her one last time, and his sweat-slicked body stilled over hers, the muscles under her hands becoming as firm as granite. Growling her name into her neck, he followed her to fulfillment.

* * * *

Abby closed the pearl snaps of his shirt and wobbled through the kitchen. She lifted the collar and breathed in Seth's scent. She loved the way he smelled and tasted.

The shirt barely covered her, but there was no way she'd walk around the house completely nude. She could only imagine what he'd think of her pudgy belly and full hips if he'd taken the time to actually look at her. She turned on the light over the sink and filled a glass with water.

She swallowed the cold sip and closed her eyes. What had she done?

"Hey, I came back from the bathroom to find you gone." Seth entered from the hall, running his fingers through his tousled hair, and as nude as the day as he was born. Her gaze traveled over his amazing body, and he watched her as if unable to get enough of her either.

He sauntered toward her and wrapped his arms around her. "Damn. Too bad Urban's already done that one."

"What's that?"

"You look good in my shirt," he said, referring to a Keith Urban hit song. "But you look even better without it."

Heat warmed her cheeks, and she leaned up to place a kiss on his lips. "You just plain look good...period."

He removed the glass from her hand and took a sip before setting it on the counter. When he responded to her, she moaned and lifted her leg, bringing herself intimately against him. How could she be so achy for him so soon?

He raised a brow. "You haven't been anywhere near loved enough, if you can still look at me like that."

"Like what?"

"Like you want to eat me right up."

"Maybe I do."

"Good. Because I'm feeling a little famished myself." He lifted her, and she wrapped her legs around his waist. She wiggled against his erection. Chuckling low and sensually in her ear, he carried her back to bed. "Trust me, this will definitely be better than chocolate cake."

"It already is."

* * * *

Seth awoke from the deepest sleep he'd had in a long time, but dawn was another two hours away. Abby lay curled against his side, warm and soft. Her breathing was gentle and sated, her hair tangled around her shoulders and over the pillowcase.

His heart constricted at her beauty in the silvery starlight from the window. He wasn't sure who seduced whom last night. The evening started out as planned. He'd wine and dine her, make her feel something for him, and then he'd be set. He'd have the in he wanted to get her to agree to tell Emily the truth.

The one thing he'd feared most with this plan had happened.

He'd fallen completely and utterly in love with her all over again.

But he wasn't sure if she felt anything for him. She hadn't professed her feelings for him; she hadn't given him a clue at all concerning her hopes for a future. The same magic simmered around them as it had the night Emily had been conceived, but she hadn't loved him then.

It was just sex... Seth, I don't love you.

Her words from the night he'd wanted her to go with him drilled through his heart.

Would she regret last night? Was it just a repeat of that night fifteen years ago?

He couldn't face the answers.

Did you love Mike?

Yes.

Brushing his fingers over the side of her cheek, he whispered, "Do you still love him?"

His answer was her turning away from him in her sleep.

He put his arms behind his head and stared at the ceiling. He was a fool. Always had been when it came to Abby, but now it wasn't just her involved. Nothing had changed his desire regarding being Emily's father.

He glanced over at her shapely shoulder and back. He'd never awakened to a woman beside him in the morning light. Staying always signified something more than just a night of pleasure. Staying meant sharing a toothbrush and breakfast. Staying meant regrets.

He couldn't deal with staring across the breakfast table at Abby's regrets reflecting in her brandy eyes.

Careful not to disturb her, he tossed off the covers and quickly pulled on his jeans and boots. She'd put his shirt on after they'd taken a shower together sometime after one, but it was warm enough he didn't need it to drive back to Johanna's house.

He'd never get the memory of her out of it anyway.

* * * *

The bright sunlight through the window awakened Abby slowly. Moaning, she sat up and glanced at the empty side of the bed. On the pillow, in the indent where Seth's head had lain, were a single red rose and a folded scrap of paper.

She picked up the rose and smelled it. The sweetness couldn't cover the spicy musk of his cologne or the underlying maleness of him. Taking a deep breath, she opened the small sheet of paper.

Call me. I want to see you again. S

She stared at the bold, blocky writing and smelled the rose again. Sweet mercy, had he made love to her three times? The last time had been against the wall in the shower. She couldn't even count how many times she'd climaxed. Sighing like a woman who had been well and thoroughly loved, she lay back on the rumpled bed.

The smile faded, and she glanced at the note again. He didn't love her. If last night hadn't been just another one-night stand to him, he wouldn't have left. Wasn't that what she'd read in *Cosmo* and all those romance novels--not staying signaled the one leaving didn't want anything permanent?

"What am I to you, Seth? Just another friend with benefits?"

Closing her eyes, she pulled the rose and note to her chest, hugging his shirt close to her body. She knew better than to want more. Did he want more than a one-night-stand?

She sat up and looked at the rose and note. He wanted her to call him. Maybe he didn't want to be gone this morning when his aunt woke up. It was time to tell Emily the truth, because she wanted more.

"Can we possibly have a future together?"

Chapter 9

"What the hell do you mean, you aren't coming back to Nashville next week?" The whiny voice of Seth's manager sounded in his ear. "We had a deal, Seth. One month. Your month is up."

He gripped his cell phone so hard his hand hurt. "I don't really give a flying fuck about what you have planned, Gary. I can't leave yet."

"You're talking about screwing over the *Late Show*! I also have feelers out to promote the new single on *Good Morning America* and other places. Amanda's on board. All we need is you to show up."

He paced the aunt's living room, gritting his teeth and fighting the urge to toss his fancy-assed smart phone through a window. "Look. I know I said one month, but something's come up here and I can't leave. Tell Amanda's people I'm sorry, but we'll have to just wait for the CMAs to sing the song live together."

The last thing he wanted to do right now was sing a love song with Amanda Lang. They'd gotten the idea to do a song last year after several of their colleagues had huge successes with pop-country crossover songs. But Abby would never understand if he ran off to New York to sing with his ex-girlfriend.

If she cared at all.

He couldn't believe she didn't.

"What is wrong with you? You'd never blow a chance like this."

"I'm in the process of buying my father's ranch." He stared out the front window at the street. "And my aunt needs me right now. She doesn't have any other family. Dad's death was hard on her."

His manager's labored breathing hissed in his ear. He could imagine the man beating the end of a cigarette on his desk. "All right. All fucking right."

Seth released the tension in his jaw. Gary was such a sucker when it came to old aunts. He'd been raised by his.

"But I sure as hell don't like it."

"You don't have to like it. I'll call Amanda personally to apologize. I think I know a way to placate her. You make things square with her people."

"Don't you worry that pretty little head about a thing." A click of a lighter sounded over the line and then the hiss of air being sucked in. Gary lighting another death stick. If Seth had been there with him in person, he would've ended up with a face full of smoke when Gary spoke again. "I'll just have to kiss some major ass, but what do you care?"

He laughed, the tension leaving him. "That's why you make seven figures a year. You're good at ass kissing."

"You just get the hell back here by the beginning of October. You got it?"

"Adios." Seth hung up before Gary had the chance to get the last word in or be able to hold him to any promises.

"What was that all about? Sounded important."

He turned to Johanna standing in the doorway with a cup of coffee in each hand. When the phone in his hand started playing Jason Aldean's *Crazy Town*, he looked at the caller ID. Gary. He turned off the cell and shoved it into his pocket.

"Nope."

She handed him one of the steaming cups. "That's not how I perceived it. That was your manager, right?

He sighed. No fooling Johanna. She had ears like a bat and the intuition of a fortuneteller. Nodding, he motioned for her to have a seat on her chair, while he sat on the couch. "He wants me to be in New York by Thursday."

"And you're not going?"

He looked into the black liquid in the flowery mug. "No. I told Tammy Jo McAllister I'd sing at Founder's Day. My band is driving down a few days earlier."

"Well, that should draw a big crowd. I'm surprised it's not all over town."

"I asked her to keep my performing a surprise for the town."

"Ahh... Bet she hated that."

"She did." He tipped his mug back and gulped a big swallow of Johanna's strong brew.

"My lips are sealed. How was your date with Abby last night?" She sipped her coffee and watched him with those razor sharp blue eyes. "I'm assuming it went well. You didn't come sneaking in until four thirty this morning. What I don't get is why you left her."

He sat back and laughed. It was easier than to admit he was wondering the same damned thing. "Aunt Johanna, how can you be all dressed in your Sunday finest to head to church and ask me a question like that?"

"All right. I know when you're avoiding the issue. But you can't avoid what you feel for her forever." She smiled, stood, and ambled out of the room with her dress swishing around her legs.

Damn, Aunt, how the hell do you do always know what I'm thinking?

* * * *

Abby turned away from the sink as the kitchen door opened. Emily set her cat carrier on the floor and opened the door to let out the squalling tomcat. As she soothed Goldie, Mike entered and set Emily's suitcase by the door. He smiled at Abby, but his gaze turned hard when he noticed the bouquet of roses on the table behind her.

Emily stood from smoothing Goldie's ruffled fur and turned toward her. She hugged her, but quickly let go and headed for the table. "Oh, Momma! Are these from Seth? Is he here?"

"No. We went out last night." She swallowed and glanced at Mike.

He scowled and folded his arms over his dress shirt. "We wondered why you weren't in church this morning."

"I didn't get home until late last night." She lifted her chin, defying him to say more on the matter.

Emily hugged her again and beamed. "Wow! So, it's official. You and Seth are dating?"

Not wanting to admit that she wasn't sure what was going on, she shrugged.

Emily bounced on her toes and faced Mike. She gave him a big hug and kissed his cheek. "'Bye, Daddy."

Mike hugged her back and said into her hair, "Love you, sweetheart."

Pulling back, she smiled. "Love you, too." Emily moved away and headed down the hallway, her cat following her. "C'mon, Goldie. I can't wait to tell the girls about Mom and Seth!"

Once the bedroom door closed down the hall, Abby moved toward the coffee maker on the counter. "Would you like some coffee?"

"How many times do I have to ask you not to do this?"

She poured a cup of coffee and sipped it before facing him. "And I told you Emily and Seth have a right to get to know each other."

He bore down on her, and his face darkened. "She better never find out the truth."

"Maybe she deserves the truth, Mike." She set the cup on the counter and braced her arms behind her. "Maybe we should never have kept it a secret to begin with. Hell, I should never have married you. I should've gone with Seth when he asked me to."

He jerked back. "You'd tell her you lied?"

"Yes. I think the three of us should sit down and tell her what happened."

"No." He grabbed her arm and pulled her toward him. "I won't let you destroy my life. All I've ever asked of you is that you never tell anyone the truth."

She narrowed her eyes on him and jerked free. "Why is that, Mike? What are you so damned afraid of? I know it won't be easy on anyone. Your parents will be devastated. Emily will probably rebel against us, and things will be strained for all of us. But, damn it, Seth is her father," she ground out in a low voice. "And if he and I have a future together, it's about time I'm honest with the world."

He sucked in a breath. "I will not go along with this. Go ahead and confess your sins, but I'll tell the world how you tricked me into believing she was mine and I was duty bound to marry you."

His glare turned into an icy smile that caused her heart to freeze and fall into her stomach.

"I'll call a reporter friend of mine right now," he said. "I'm sure all the tabloids would love this story. The daughter of a disgraced preacher and an Amarillo whore follows in her mother's footsteps. Only this time, the scandal wouldn't just be a local one, it will involve one of America's biggest stars."

She flinched as if he'd hit her. How could Mike do this to her? "You wouldn't stoop that low."

He leaned in and his jaw worked as he clenched his teeth. "Try me. I know what the town thinks of you, Abby. I was cornered just this morning by Allan Marshall. He's concerned about Trevor's growing feelings toward Emily. He sugarcoated it to sound like it was their age difference, but I knew the truth."

Glenda Marshall's hateful words came back to her from the other day. *"Like mother like daughter. Your mother was a whore who lured a man of God in with her debauchery. You destroyed Mike's life. I won't allow your daughter to trap Trevor in the same snare."*

"Emily has a chance at a great future. Once she goes to college and gets a career, she can leave this town and never look back." He turned at the door and smiled. "Or you can destroy her future by telling her about how you lied to her. And I'll tell the world how you betrayed me."

When he slammed the door on his way out, she jumped and shoved her fist into her mouth to keep in the sob. She turned to stare out the window over the sink as the tears fell. How could Mike do this? He'd been her friend ever since she was a toddler in diapers.

When they started school, Mike and Seth became her protectors, her best friends, and her confidantes.

Grief battered her heart at the loss of one of her closest companions. Mike was no longer her protector, no longer her friend. He was nothing but a bully.

The phone rang, but she ignored it. She grabbed a paper towel and wetted it with cold water. Emily couldn't see her like this.

As she wiped at her eyes, Emily called from her room, "Mom! It's for you."

"Oh. I got it." Her hand shook as she picked up the receiver from the wall-mounted phone by the door. "Hello?"

"Abby, it's Jenny Lynn."

She closed her eyes at the sound of her friend's tired voice. "What's going on?"

Jenny Lynn cleared her throat on the other end. "Max Martinez passed away a few moments ago. I knew you'd want to know."

She leaned against the wall. "How's Darlene holding up?"

"As well as can be expected. I'm with her now."

She sniffed and wiped her nose. "Let me figure out what I can do with Emily, and I'll be right over."

"Thanks. You're such a great friend."

"Yeah."

* * * *

"Thanks for letting Emily hang out over here." Abby rubbed her bare arms. When she avoided meeting Seth's eyes, his heart fell.

She'd called him twenty minutes ago to ask if Emily could stay with him while she went to Amarillo. He'd come out to the ranch after Johanna went off to church. First, he'd taken a ride, then come back to the house to work on boxing up his father's life.

"She can come over here anytime she wants." He moved a cardboard box from the sofa to a chair next to the mantle. A sheen of dust covered five generations of faded photos crowding the oak plank.

She nodded and looked everywhere but at his face. "You're getting this place cleaned up."

"It's coming along." Actually, he'd not even started. He shrugged and shoved his hands into his pockets. The air conditioner kicked in, and a blast of cool air caused the hair on his arms to stand up. He wasn't sure what was colder--the air or Abby.

So, she regretted last night. At least, she wasn't keeping Emily from him.

"When do you think you'll be home?"

She looked down at her clasped hands in front of her. "I don't know. Darlene is one of the best friends I have. I'll stay with her as long as she needs me."

"Emily will be safe with me. We can stay here tonight or I can go back to your place."

"Oh, I didn't even think about tonight." She winced and combed her fingers through her hair, bringing it over her left shoulder. His hand itched to smooth over the silky strands. "At least, tomorrow is Labor Day so there's no school."

Emily entered the living room. She made her way around the room, skimming her fingertips over the antique furniture. Her bottom lip caught between her teeth.

He turned to Abby. "Why don't I go back to your place? I can sleep on the couch."

She glanced at Emily. "I can't ask you to do that."

"I want to do this. Your friend needs you." *I want to spend the time with my daughter.*

"Why not just sleep in Mom's room?" Emily stopped beside the couch, looked from her mother to him. She smiled and sat on the dusty cushion.

Nodding, Abby finally met his eyes, and he held her gaze. "Okay, make yourself at home."

If she didn't come back, he was in for a long night. No way could he sleep in her bed without the memories of last night keeping him up.

He tried to read the secrets lurking behind her brandy irises, but couldn't.

Emily leaned over her legs and rested her chin in her hand, watching them. "Just for the record, I'm happy you two are dating."

He waited for Abby's response. When she didn't speak, he said, "Me, too."

She swallowed and faced Emily. "Call me if you need anything."

Emily stood and hugged her mother. "I'll be fine. Tell Mrs. Martinez I'm sorry about her husband."

"I will." Abby gave him one last look and left.

Once the front door closed, Emily rubbed her hands together. "What do you want me to do?"

He looked around the room. Johanna had taken a few things already, but crap still crowded every nook and cranny of the old house. "Well, I figured we could start boxing up the photos. I want to keep them."

"What about the knick-knacks and the furniture?"

"An auction company is coming in later this week to pack the rest up."

"Oh. So, when are you moving in?"

He shrugged and grabbed the bundle of newspapers he'd confiscated from his aunt's stash. "I signed the papers Friday, so I could move in anytime. But I'm going to gut the place and remodel it first."

"Don't you have to go back to Nashville and get your stuff?" Emily took a sheet of paper from the pile and picked up a miniature portrait.

"Soon. But I'm fine for now." He reached for one of the photos.

She glanced at the painting in her hand and touched the ornate, rounded frame with the tip of her finger. "Who are all these people?"

He set the frame in his hand on the mantel and sighed. "My family." Pointing to the painting she held, he said, "Those are my great-great grandparents--Anna and Jack Kendall."

"I can't believe they are all sitting here. Most people have boxes of old pictures but never display them."

He leaned onto the back of the wingchair and put his hands in his pockets. "Granny Kendall insisted these stay here. Johanna told me she even dug a few out of the attic and had them framed."

She pointed to the large portrait hanging above the fireplace. "Who's that guy? He looks constipated."

He laughed and wrapped his arm around her shoulder. He studied the hard stare of his great-great-great grandfather's blue eyes. Something warm drifted through his veins at the thought of teaching Emily about her roots, even if she didn't know they were her ancestors. "I used to think so, too. That's Kit Kendall."

She looked up at him, and he met her gaze. "Was he really a gunslinger?"

He narrowed his eyes on her in surprise. "How do you know that?"

"Your dad. He told me all sorts of things about this place."

Oh, Dad, did you enjoy Emily as much as I am? He pulled his gaze from hers and looked at the painting. "He rode with Jesse James during the War Between the States and was quite the outlaw after the war. Until he met his wife Maggie and found religion. Then they moved to Texas and bought this spread." He pointed to a smaller portrait between the front windows. "That's her over there."

She scrunched up her brow and stared at the portrait of the tiny, dark-haired woman. "Why wasn't he ever hung for his crimes, if he was so bad?"

He squeezed her shoulders, and she looked up at him again. "I often wondered the same thing. Story goes that he was never caught. My guess is he wasn't as bad as the stories say he was."

She nodded and stepped away. "What are you gonna do with all these pictures?"

Needing to do something with his hands, he wrapped a photo and gently put it into the box. "I'm going to donate them to the historical society. And I'm going to keep some of them. Like old Kit and Maggie, there."

She put the miniature painting in the box. "That's cool."

They worked for several minutes until Emily picked up a photo and stared at it for a long time. "Who's this?"

His breath caught in his throat. "My grandfather and grandmother-- Aaron and Kathleen Kendall. Dad's and Johanna's parents."

The picture had been taken during World War II and was black and white, but there was no denying the uncanny resemblance between the newlywed girl in the photo and the teenager holding it.

"She's pretty." Emily grabbed paper and wrapped the photo.

"I always thought so."

If she recognized the similarity in herself with the woman long dead, Emily didn't let on. He wasn't sure if he was relieved or disappointed.

He cleared his throat. "Do you know what you'll sing for Founder's Day? It's only three weeks away."

She set the photo in the box and shrugged. "I think so. Tammy Jo said she was going to talk to you about singing too."

"Yeah, she asked me."

"What did you say?"

He rubbed his hand against his thigh. "Can you keep a surprise?"

"Yeah." Her eyes brightened.

"I'll be there, and I have a special guest flying in too. She and my band will be here a few days before the show."

"She?"

"That's a surprise." He touched his finger to her nose and smiled.

He hoped having Amanda show up here along with a camera crew would make everyone happy. They'd get the exposure they needed for the new single. He'd pitched the idea to Amanda earlier, she agreed, and he'd called Gary again. His manager thought giving up the national exposure in New York was crazy, but he liked the idea of using the backdrop of his hometown to shoot a video. Gary was lining up a producer to fly in sometime next week to get things under way.

What he hoped to get out of it all was Abby realizing the other singer meant nothing to him.

Emily bounced on her feet and threw her arms around his waist. "Yay! I don't care as long as you're singing."

He held her for a moment and just breathed her in. Now, if he could just figure out what was up with Abby, life might actually be pretty darned good.

* * * *

Abby hadn't seen much of Seth over the rest of the week except when he visited the nursing home or when they spent time together with Emily in the evenings. She'd taken on a few extra hours and worked during the days while Emily was in school. They hadn't had time alone to really talk.

On Friday, she rounded a corner after passing the morning medicines, to find Seth waiting by the nursing station. He tapped his fingers on countertop as he leaned over the shelf surrounding the station. The man screamed *sexy* in his tight faded jeans and black t-shirt.

She went behind the counter and started typing away on the computer.

The fingers stopped tapping on the shelf. "Can we talk?"

She shook her head. "I'm busy. We got a new resident, and she's raising all kinds of heck. And I'm short a nurse and an aide."

"You've been busy all week. So, I have plans for after you get off work tonight."

As she stopped typing, she looked up at him. "Emily--"

"Emily will be with Carolann and Frank. I've already talked to them. They're going to take her with them to visit Mary Jane down in Dallas for the weekend," he said, referring to Mike's younger, globetrotting sister. "So, you have no excuse. On Sunday, she goes with Mike. Everything, including your work schedule, has been taken care of."

She sighed and leaned back in her chair. She bit her bottom lip. God, she wanted to spend time with him. "What do you have planned?"

"Something special." When she started to shake her head, he added, "All you need to do is say yes. And pack enough for a two-day trip. Although, I doubt you'll need any of it."

"I'm not going anywhere with you. I have the ranch--"

"You can go willingly or I'll kidnap you. The choice is yours. I talked to Judd, and he'll take care of the ranch in your absence," he countered, referring to her foreman.

"You thought of everything." Excitement curled in her lower belly at the way he grinned at her. A whole weekend with the one thing she couldn't have, but wanted beyond all reason. Maybe she could convince herself that he only wanted sex and couldn't possibly feel anything for her.

Or she could fall even deeper in love with him, become even more miserable than she already was.

"I am a thinker."

She laughed and stood up. "Okay, I'll go with you. But I'm not leaving the state of Texas."

"That still leaves me with a ton of possibilities. Texas is a damned big state."

She came around the counter, took his hand and led him to the elevator. She hugged herself, but would rather have hugged him. Since Saturday night, she couldn't stop thinking about him. "I'm only going with you because we do need to talk, and it's hard to do with Emily around."

"You sound so serious."

"I am."

The time had come to come clean about her and Mike's marriage. He'd threatened her again about going to the tabloids if she continued to see Seth. However, she sensed something in Seth over the past few days that gave her heart hope.

Was she foolish to think he would forgive her and they had a future together?

He touched her cheek, and she leaned into the caress. "I'll pick you up at five."

"I'll be ready."

But was she ready for Mike to drag her, Emily and Seth into the dirt?

Chapter 10

Abby stepped out of the bathroom of the rented cabin, wearing hot pink, silk boy shorts, a matching floral chemise and nothing else. Sexy boxer briefs rode decadently low on the hips and hugged the tight behind of the man taking up more than his share of the space in front of the indoor grill. Her heart sped up as she admired Seth's bare wide shoulders, muscular back and long, toned legs before she moved in behind him to wrap her arms around him.

True to his word, he'd shown up that evening ready to whisk Abby away. She'd refused to go until he admitted where he planned to take her. He'd relented and announced he'd booked a weekend stay at a cabin in the park at the Palo Duro Canyon.

He'd come down while she'd been at work to get everything ready. The far-from-quaint, not-too-rustic cabin was perfect. Candlelight lit up the place. A red-checkered tablecloth covered the small round table, and in the middle sat a vase of deep red roses. He'd definitely put a lot of thought into this little surprise.

"I wondered when you'd stop admiring the view." He put two steaks on the grill.

"Nothing's wrong with your ego."

He glanced over his shoulder at her and gave her a sexy-as-sin grin. "Nope."

When he laughed, Abby swatted his shoulder. She looked around his shoulder at the delicious smelling T-bones. "Where'd you learn to cook?"

"I'm a bachelor. I either had to learn to cook or starve."

She laughed as she began to caress his bare, hard belly, her fingers inching lower over a six-pack like bands of steel under tanned skin. "Well, we wouldn't want you to starve."

He chuckled, and the rumbling sound spread fire over her skin. The sensation of his vibrating back against her sensitive breasts caused her to bite back a moan. She dipped her hand lower and cupped his hardening erection.

He groaned and pushed her hands away. "You'd better stop or I'll overcook the steaks."

"Maybe I'm not in the mood for steaks." Her belly took that inopportune moment to growl.

"Huh-uh. Tell that to the lion in there. I know you haven't eaten much today, and I need you to be well nourished for what I've got planned."

She kept her gaze locked on his as she kissed his shoulder. "Maybe I'll just take a bite…" She paused to nip the skin she'd kissed. "Out of you. You look pretty darned yummy."

He growled and seemed close to giving in. She relented because she was hungry for food as well as for the man. As she moved away from him to wash her hands at the sink, she asked, "So what is on the menu, besides T-bones, Chef Seth?"

He raised a brow at her. "You're the assistant. The fridge is stocked." Inside the small refrigerator were three bottles of very expensive wine, including a bottle of Dom Perignon. Brie cheese, green grapes and strawberries also took up space in the small compartment, but what she pulled out were romaine lettuce, a cucumber and a green pepper. Cherry tomatoes were on the counter.

She quickly turned the vegetables into a salad on the small counter space next to the stove. "So, you brought me down here to talk. What are we talking about?"

He flipped the steaks and glanced at her. "We'll get to it eventually."

She nodded and looked down at the green pepper she was julienning. "Maybe it would be better if we talked sooner."

He turned to face her. "What's going on, Abby? You obviously want me, or you wouldn't be here."

She dumped the peppers into the bowl and gave the mixture a toss with her hands. As she wiped her hands on a towel, she said, "I have a confession to make."

He raised a brow and folded his arms over that amazing expanse of chest. "Go ahead."

She mentally shook herself and couldn't admit the truth about her and Mike's marriage. Turned away, she evenly filled two salad bowls. "Let's eat first."

His brows puckered, but he dropped his arms and went back to tending the meat. "Okay."

He plated the steaks and pulled the bottle of champagne from the fridge.

Once they were seated, Seth popped the cork on the Dom Perignon. White foam bubbled out of the opening. He grabbed the two champagne flutes and poured them both full of the sparkling wine.

He was so different now--sophisticated and knowledgeable in things that she didn't even understand. The Seth from before wouldn't have known the difference between Dom Perignon and the sour stuff Mike's grandfather had made from the scrawny grapes he grew out on the Circle R.

Yet, he was the same boy who had pulled the frilly ribbons from her pigtails and had played high school football when he wasn't fooling around with his guitar.

She took the glass he offered and touched the rim to his. "So, what are we toasting?"

His grin got sexier, and he tapped her glass. "What else? To us."

"To us."

They returned the champagne glasses to the table, and he picked up his fork and poked at his salad. Silence ensued for a few moments, with neither of them eating much of the meal before them. With a sigh, he set his fork down and peered at her. "What's going on, Abby?"

She wiped her mouth on the white napkin, closed her eyes and took a deep breath. "My marriage to Mike wasn't what you think it was." She met his troubled gaze and clenched the napkin in her lap. "I never loved Mike. At least not in the way a wife should love her husband."

He sat straight, and his shoulders and jaw tensed. "What are you saying?"

She shook her head and tried to get air into her constricted lungs. "I was afraid. Mike never left my side after you left. He knew how scared I was. Daddy was dying and most people figured he'd gotten what he deserved. He was a preacher who regularly visited a prostitute, after all. Then had the gall to marry her when she got pregnant. I was afraid what people would say about me. But mostly, I didn't want people to think badly of you, so I never told anyone who the father was."

"Mike convinced you to marry him."

She sniffed and fought the urge to let the tears go. Nodding, she looked up into the dark face of the only man she'd ever loved. "Yeah. At first, I didn't want to do it. I didn't want to trap him into a marriage with a woman he didn't love. I knew he was feeling jilted by Tammy Jo. She'd dumped him before she went off to Harvard."

"What changed your mind?" The pain in his low, jagged voice ripped at her heart.

"I watched your performance with Amanda Lang on that talent show. The way you looked at her when you sang together. You looked like you were in love with her. She hung all over you. Then I heard you two were dating."

* * * *

Seth forced the tension to leave his jaw so he could speak. A tear streaked a wet trail from her pain-filled eyes. His own pain turned his guts to knots. "It was an act, Abby. I never loved Amanda. Hell, I didn't even like her all that much. She was my biggest competition, and I wanted to beat her. The media saw what you did and jumped to conclusions that were not true."

She wiped at the tear. "How was I supposed to know? You never called. You didn't even write to me. I figured you realized what a liability I'd be. What our baby would be."

"Liability?"

"I'm half Indian, Seth. Country music has never been very tolerant of different races. Then there's the scandal surrounding my parents. I figured you realized what I'd always known. I'd only hurt your career."

Her words flattened him. When he could breathe, he forced out, "That's why you didn't go with me."

"Yes." The strangled word came with a wash of tears.

"Jesus, Abby." He pushed away from the table, pulled her out of her chair and held her.

She burrowed into him. Her tears were hot on his chest. "I didn't want you to lose your chance. I knew how much it meant to you to win. How much you wanted to be a singer."

He kissed her temple and squeezed his eyes shut.

"But Mike only married me for my money. He's threatening me, Seth."

He held her away and stared down into her red, tearful eyes. "How?"

She sniffed and wiped at her nose with the back of her hand. "If we tell Emily the truth about you being her father, he's going to go to a tabloid and say I tricked him."

"That slimy bastard." She jumped at the harshness of his voice, and he pulled her back to him. "Tammy Jo doesn't know the truth. I'd bet my record deal that she never dumped him. She probably didn't want to marry him right out of high school, but he needed money fast to save the Circle R."

She nodded against his shoulder. "Right after we were married he asked me to tap into the money Daddy won in the settlement after the accident. Daddy never touched the money. He called it blood money. Anyway, I used it to pay the back taxes on the Circle R."

"How much did you sink into the ranch?"

"Most of it. I have enough to send Emily to college but that's about it, and most of that I've saved over the years."

Rage, hot and feral, spread through his veins. "That's why you work at the nursing home. Just to make ends meet."

"I don't know why he's doing this. I know he loves Emily, but you being in her life doesn't have to change his relationship with her."

"Maybe not, but it would affect his relationship with his rich new wife."

She looked up at him. Her eyes were red and swollen, and he hated what this had done to all of them--her, him, and most of all, Emily.

"What are we going to do, Seth?"

"Don't you worry about Mike." He feathered his fingers over her cheek. "But we have to tell Emily the truth."

She nodded and laid her hand over his heart. "She also has to know you didn't abandon her."

"What do you mean?"

She closed her eyes again and shivered. "I know what Mike told you the day you came back after she was born. I'm sorry. I should have known you wouldn't abandon her."

"Baby..." He'd never hated Mike Ritter more than he did at that moment. They were both victims of his malicious lies.

He held her for a long moment until she stopped crying. "I hope you already know this, but I've wanted to tell you something for a long time." She met his gaze. He rubbed his thumbs over the wet tracks on her cheeks and swallowed hard. "I love you, Abby. I always have."

* * * *

The words seeped through Abby, making her head spin and her heart as light as a sunbeam. "I love you, too," she whispered, stunned at the intensity in his beautiful eyes. "I wish I'd known how you felt."

"I almost didn't go to Nashville that night. I left your ranch and went to our place by the lake. I sat there until morning. I couldn't believe you didn't love me."

Her heart crashed into the pit of her stomach, and a new gush of tears burned her eyes. "I shouldn't have lied to you."

Seth's eyes were shadowed. The stormy pain in their depths battered at the thin dam of her resolve.

He might love her, but he'd never forgive her.

She stepped away and glanced at the cooling dinner on the table. "We should probably eat before everything gets cold."

He rubbed at his beard and nodded. "Yeah."

They sat down, and he avoided looking at her. He picked up the wine glass and twirled the champagne before tossing it back in one gulp.

Looking for a way to change the subject to something not as charged, she sipped from her glass. The champagne hit her stomach and soured. "So tell me, when did you start drinking two-hundred-dollars-a-bottle champagne?"

He was quiet so long she didn't expect him to answer. She lowered her head and picked up the fork beside her plate. His voice was low and brought her gaze back to his. "When my first album was certified gold, Gary Russell bought me a bottle to celebrate. I bought him a bottle when my third single, *Only a Memory* hit the top of the charts. He was one of the few people who believed in that song. It proved I could write as well as sing."

They sat in silence for several more minutes, both of them playing with their food, but neither of them eating.

She set her fork on her plate and picked up her wine glass. As she looked into the slightly amber liquid, she said, "I'll never forget the first time I heard it. I was driving Emily to the doctor for a checkup when the DJ came on and said that he'd just got a new single in from you."

"What was wrong with Emily?"

She blinked and met his narrowed eyes. "Oh, nothing. It was just a well-child visit. She was scheduled to get an immunization. That's all."

"She wasn't sick?"

His concern made her sinuses burn. "No, but I almost missed the appointment. I still get goose bumps when I think of hearing you on the radio back then. I had to pull over because I started crying. I was just so damned proud of you."

He looked away, but not before she caught the shadowy emotion in his eyes. What it meant, she couldn't tell.

She grabbed her chest at the bitter-sweetness of the memory. "It took me twenty minutes to get myself under control after the DJ announced your name. But in those twenty minutes, the radio station buzzed with people calling in about the song and about you. They loved you, and I knew I'd made the right choice. I would've only held you back."

He swallowed so hard his throat moved, and his voice dipped low. "After it was released, I often wondered if you ever got its meaning."

"I think maybe I've always known it was about us, but convinced myself it wasn't. It was easier that way."

"Why?"

"Because I never wanted to admit I might have been wrong. I didn't want to admit I've always loved you."

Seth laid his fork down and tossed back his second glass of champagne. He picked up his plate and headed to the sink, dumped his uneaten dinner in the garbage and set the plate in the sink with a clank.

* * * *

Abby had admitted to loving him, but it hadn't made him feel any better. If anything, her admission made things worse. She'd lied to him.

He braced his arms against the edge of the sink and leaned over them. The scrape of her chair against the plank floor grated against his ragged nerves. Damn, he shouldn't want her so much. His entire body was on fire with need. He shouldn't love her so much his heart ached.

But he did.

When she moved in beside him, he closed his eyes against the floral scent of her skin. "Why did you lie to me about your feelings?"

The implications of her confession hung heavy in the air between them.

"I knew you'd stay. And I knew it would've destroyed you. But I couldn't go with you for the same reason. Even if you would've married me. I wasn't even eighteen yet. What would all those people out there who voted for you, who supported the clean-cut Texas kid, have thought of you then?"

"Damn it, Abby! I loved you." He turned to look at her.

She leaned her backside against the counter and met his gaze with eyes full of painful regret. She'd known him better than anyone. She knew about his mother and his fear of becoming like her. He didn't agree with her reasoning for not going with him, but he understood why she'd think the way she did. The people of McAllister never had much tolerance for her. Why would she think the rest of the world would be any different?

He'd show her they had a future. Show her how much he loved her. Moving away from the sink, he wrapped his hand around the back of her head. He pulled her to him and possessed her lips with a kiss meant to claim her, to brand her.

Her hands went around him to his ass, clenching at his flesh through his boxer briefs. She tasted of champagne and salty tears when she opened her mouth under his. He groaned and ran his free hand over the silk of her top to cup her breast. Her nipple hardened under his fingers as she arched into his touch.

He plunged his tongue deep into her sweet mouth. Her tongue caressed his and dueled with him. She pressed her soft curves into his over-sensitive erection and ground against him. When she slipped her hands under his waistband and scraped her fingernails over his bare skin, his cock went beyond hard.

He growled and grabbed her top. Breaking the kiss, he pulled it over her head. She pushed his briefs over his hips, and he yanked her sexy little shorts to the floor. With the side of his hand, he shoved the dishes off the counter into the sink with a clang of broken glass and lifted her onto the edge.

He slid his lips over her chin to her neck, stopped to suckle at the racing pulse, then rained nipping kisses down to her breast. The dark brown peaks stood atop beautiful full breasts. He sucked in one of the luscious buds and fingered the other one.

She arched her back, and her head lolled to the side when he scraped his teeth over the rock-hard pebbles. Her legs surrounded him and pulled him closer. "Seth..."

Deep in his soul, he heard the plea in her breathy call. With love and desire for her, he'd do anything to please her. Slipping his lips over her belly, he knelt before her, then draped her long, shapely legs over his shoulders. He looked up into her passion-darkened eyes and parted the dark curls covering her weeping sex.

* * * *

Abby fisted her fingers into Seth's hair as he placed open-mouthed, sucking kisses over her inner thigh to her most intimate place. His lips and the brush of his beard on her were pure decadence. He flicked his tongue over her, and she cried out at the jolt of sweet pleasure. Her breathing hitched when his hands stroked up her body to cover and knead her breasts. As he rolled her hard nipples between his fingers, he suckled her, taking her to a place so high she couldn't breathe.

When the orgasm started, she gasped and screamed his name. Grasping at his hair with her hands and tightening her hold on him with her legs, she didn't want to let the pleasure go. She didn't want to let him go.

The last shudder quaked through her, and her sated body relaxed. She opened her eyes and her cheeks heated at the sight of him still between her legs, his green eyes bright with the fire of his own desire, and a cocky, sexy grin curving his moist lips.

"You're a wildcat, woman."

She smiled and brushed her fingers over his stubble-roughened cheek and into his wavy, silky hair. "You make me wild."

Cupping the back of his head, she bent and captured his lips. He stood, wrapped her up, and lifted her off the counter. She bit his bottom lip and thrilled at her power when he growled low in his chest. He caught her tongue and sucked, and then thrust his deep into her mouth in direct imitation of what she wanted him to do to her.

By the time they made their way into the alcove holding a king-sized bed, she was breathless, the ache to have him inside her unbearable.

He laid her on the soft mattress, reached for a condom from the shelf beside the bed and sheathed himself. She pulled him over her, and his lips found hers again. As he cupped her breast, his thumb maddeningly fanned the sensitive nipple.

She moaned, moved her hand between them to his long, thick erection. She stroked him with one hand while her nails raked his back, pulling him to her. He rose over her and stared down at her.

The love she saw in his hungry eyes filled her with deep and overwhelming joy. She'd never felt anything so profound before. He lifted her legs and draped them over his shoulders. When he filled her with a single, powerful thrust, the sense of completion, the connection so intimately shared with this beautiful man, almost shattered her.

He pulled the whole way out and pounded into her, deeper than before. Each thrust came quicker than the one before until he set a frantic rhythm.

He tossed his head back and gritted his teeth as her orgasm washed over her, hot, wild, and amazing. She met him thrust for thrust, her inner muscles grasping him and pulling him deeper with each turbulent wave. As she'd expected the storm to subside, she gasped when the sensations swept her higher than before.

Her cry of ecstasy matched his shout of triumph as she tumbled over the pinnacle again--this time, taking him with her.

She'd never give him up without a fight and would do anything to keep him by her side.

Chapter 11

"I met with an architect Frank recommended and a contractor Tucker Cowley suggested, yesterday." He took Abby's hand and led her around the house on the Double K to the backyard. "If we can believe the contractor, he said he'll have the renovation done by the end of November."

Maybe by then he'd know if they had a future.

God, he hoped so.

They stopped at the back of the kitchen. "What do you have planned?"

The past week had been pure bliss. He'd practically moved in with her since their return from the cabin Sunday night, but he knew it was short-lived. Emily would return Sunday, and they both agreed they had to cool things off a little when she came home.

They also planned to sit down with her Sunday evening and tell her the whole truth.

As much as he wanted her to know, the prospect scared the hell out of him.

"I'm going to completely redo the kitchen and add a studio over there." He pointed to an area at the back of the house behind the study. "Over the new addition, I'd like to add a master bedroom suite." The moment the words were out, he glanced at her.

"Sounds nice."

"I think so. I hope you'll help me with the house." He studied her and held his breath. "I'm meeting with the architect Monday to finalize my plans before he draws anything up. I'd like you to be there."

What would she say if he asked her about that future?

"I don't know how much help I'd be. I'm no good at that kind of thing."

"I'm not either. Mainly because I don't have time to be. If you'd like, I'll hire an interior decorator. I want a place to come home to after being on the road for long stretches of time."

I want to come home to you.

The wind seemed to get a whole lot colder within a heartbeat. As she folded her arms in front of her, she faced him. She was good at burning hell-fire hot one moment and polar cold the next. "How much time will you be living here if you're on the road so much?"

He shoved his hands into the pockets of his jeans. "I'll be gone a lot. I can't deny that. But I hope by adding the studio, I can do a lot of my recording here instead of having to go to Nashville."

"How much time away are we talking about?"

She wouldn't like his answer. Hell, he didn't like his answer. "At least six to eight months. I'm planning a world tour early next summer. This will be the longest time. Australia and Europe, then Canada before hitting the States again in the late fall. I'll be able to come home between dates, but those stays won't be long."

She nodded and looked over the pastures beyond the fence. Somewhere a cow lowed and a bird flew past them, making the silence stretch all the longer. "I heard your new song on the radio this morning."

That love song with Amanda. "What did you think of it?" He already had a pretty damned good idea from the way she was acting.

She shrugged and rubbed her arms. "Did you write it?"

He sighed and looked at the dirt. If he lied, she'd only learn the truth anyway. "Amanda and I, along with another Nashville writer, wrote it together."

"Oh. Will she be going on this world tour with you?"

"We're planning a few dates together in Australia in June."

Looking at her watch, she said, "I'd better get going. I have to work this evening."

"Abby." He reached over and took her by the arm to turn her toward him. "Amanda and I have a professional relationship and nothing more."

"I guess I just need to get used to that." She smiled, but it didn't fully reach her eyes.

He held her close and covered her mouth with his in a passion-laced kiss. When he finally pulled away, he feathered the back of his fingers over her cheek. "I love you, Abigail. No one else. Remember that."

She seemed to relax into him, and her smile lit her face. "I love you, too." She kissed him again before moving out of his arms. "Now, I really have to go. I'm meeting Jenny Lynn and Darlene for lunch before I have to be at work."

He walked her back to her truck. As he opened the door for her, he said, "See you tonight."

She got in and turned to him. Her eyes brightened as she cranked the engine of the big Chevy. "Definitely."

* * * *

Following Sunday church services, Emily came home with Abby and Seth. Abby had dreaded meeting Mike at church, but her mind eased when she learned he was working, which she found odd. He never worked on Sundays, and if Tammy Jo's moodiness was a good guide, she found it strange, too. Then Emily said he was at the Circle R. He had something to take care of.

The confrontation with her ex-husband didn't happen, but her nerves were raw with anxiousness. She wasn't looking forward to the conversation she should have had with her daughter a long time ago.

If Seth's tense movements and brooding as they prepared lunch together were any indication, he was as on edge as she.

She set the plate of tuna sandwiches and a salad on the table while he poured sweet tea over the ice in tall glasses. He glanced at her when Emily entered the kitchen. Her big, yellow tomcat followed and meowed at the sliding glass door. Emily let the cat out, and he plopped down in the bright sunlight on the deck.

She turned and looked from Abby to Seth. "You two look like someone died." Scrunching up her face, she shoved her hands in the back pockets of her jeans shorts. "No one died, did they?"

Abby went to Emily and wrapped her arm around her shoulders. "No. No one died." She looked at Seth. He pulled out the chair, and Abby guided her to it. "Sit down and let's eat."

With suspicious looks at both them, Emily slowly took her seat. Seth held the back of Abby's chair at the head of the table, then sat in his across from Emily, who watched them as he took one of the sandwiches and Abby filled her salad dish.

Emily ate her sandwich in silence for a few moments. "Okay." She sipped her tea and set the glass on the table with a thump "Something's going on. Seth, you've mutilated that sandwich, and Mom, if you mix that salad much more it's going to become mush."

Abby set her fork on her plate and met Seth's troubled gaze.

"Just tell me what's up with you two. You didn't run off and elope last weekend and now are afraid to tell me, did you?"

"No, sunshine. Your momma and me didn't elope." His voice was so low it rumbled through Abby's chest.

"Em, sweetheart, Seth and I do have something we need to tell you. And it won't be easy."

Emily's eyes widened a bit and her shoulders squared. She bit her lip as she looked from Abby to Seth and back again. "Sounds scary."

Seth pushed his chair back and stood, taking his plate with him. He smiled, but it never reached his eyes. "Not at all. C'mon, help me with the dishes, then we'll all have a sit-down in the living room."

Ten minutes later, her heart pounded so hard and fast she feared the beat could be heard clear to Amarillo. She sat on the couch, Emily took the chair by the piano and Seth eased in beside her on the sofa. She swallowed and looked up at him, hoping he knew how to explain their mistakes to their teenage daughter.

He took a deep breath, leaned over his long legs and rested his elbows on his thighs. As he stroked his beard, he said, "Emily, fifteen years ago your mom and me made some really stupid mistakes."

Emily sat board straight and her face went white.

Abby laid her hand on his forearm, and he met her gaze. Her mouth went dry and blood rushed in her ears when she faced her daughter. "I want you to know I've always loved you and wish I'd never done what I did."

With stark white shock draining her face, leaving the light freckles to stand out in stunning relief over her aristocratic nose she'd inherited from Seth, Emily started shaking her head.

Dear God, she'd figured it out on her own.

"That picture."

"What picture?" she asked, glancing at Seth.

"At your house." Emily stared at him. "The woman you said was your grandma... She looked a lot like me." She paused and shook her head. Her gasped, quiet words bounced off the walls in the room to echo in her throbbing head. "You're my father."

"Yes." His deep voice rasped.

"Did you know about me?"

* * * *

Acid swirled in Seth's gut. He'd wanted her to know about him being her father ever since that day she answered Carolann's door, but now he realized her knowing meant he had some explaining to do.

Explaining that didn't blame anyone else but himself.

Not Mike, not Abby, not even his parents.

He stood, moved around the coffee table and knelt before Emily. He brushed loose strands of auburn hair from her forehead. His fingers lingered, barely touching her ashen face. "I knew about you, sunshine."

She puckered her brow, and her green eyes glistened with pain, betrayal and confusion. "I don't understand. Why didn't you... Didn't you want me?"

Her quiet question stabbed him in the heart and twisted. His sinuses stung and his eyes burned. He struggled for a jagged breath. He pulled her into his arms and held her. But how did he answer her question? Yes, Abby's marriage to his best friend and Mike's words regarding his ability to be a good dad because of his parents' messed up life had led to his staying away, but he'd made a conscious decision not to be part of Emily's life.

A decision he would regret for as long as he lived.

He buried his nose into her hair, breathed the scent of strawberries and young girl, and fought the noose around his neck, but lost the battle.

"I told Seth not to be part of your life."

At Abby's tear-laced words, he looked over his shoulder at her. She met his gaze. Tears ran down her cheeks, and her face was etched with heartache.

"What?" Emily pushed away from him and looked at her mother. "Why?"

Abby knelt beside him and sniffed. "I was scared. And I loved him. The last thing I wanted to do was screw up his chance at having a music career. So, I told him to go. That--that I didn't need him or want him around." She wiped at the tears on her face and looked down at her hands. "When Mike asked me to marry him, I did. Seth came home and thought I betrayed him. I thought he'd betrayed me and neither of us was smart enough to talk about what happened."

"Does--does Daddy know?"

Abby nodded, but before she could speak, he'd had enough of her taking all the blame for his actions. "He married her to prevent her from having you alone." Emily didn't need to know Mike's real reasons. She'd figure those out on her own eventually. "She never had a good childhood, sunshine. When her mom was killed and her dad paralyzed in a car accident, he took to drinking and being mean. Your mom dealt with mean people all her life just because of her ethnicity and the mistakes of her parents." He wrapped his arm around Abby's quivering shoulders. "She thought she was protecting me."

Abby closed her eyes and shook her head. "Sweetheart--"

Again, he interrupted her. She'd inflicted enough wounds with her own sword. "And I was too easily convinced my way was the only way. I never thought I could be a good father. I probably wouldn't have been, but I was wrong to stay away. I wish I'd been here for you."

Emily stared up at him with teary, red-rimmed eyes. He laid his big hand on the side of her small face and dried her tears with his thumb.

"Why did you think you wouldn't be a good dad?"

He sniffed--damn, his sinuses burned--and shifted his weight onto his other leg. "You and my dad spent a lot of time together. Did he ever tell you how my mom died?"

She shook her head. "He just said she died a long time ago."

"My mom was a singer. When she was twenty, she sang at the rodeo over in Amarillo and a talent scout wanted her to come to Nashville. She'd just had me and married my dad. He wouldn't let her go. Dad never wanted her to be a singer."

"Why?"

He shook his head, remembering the letter. "Fear. I think. He was afraid that she'd leave him if she became famous. I'm not sure my mother ever loved my dad, but he loved her."

"How did she die?"

He swallowed hard and glanced at Abby. Her understanding and love shone in her eyes and gave him strength. "Mom committed suicide when she was twenty-three. I was a few months shy of turning five." Emily's eyes widened and he averted his gaze. "After Dad refused to let her try her luck in Nashville, she started drinking and taking drugs. She overdosed. My dad became mean and hated that I wanted to be a singer. He told me all my childhood I was just like her."

He squeezed his eyes shut. They burned like hell-fire. "When your mom told me she was pregnant with you, I was just eighteen. I had just won a spot on the talent show *America's Rising Star*."

"You were afraid you'd end up like her." Emily touched his face with cool, shaky fingers.

He snapped his gaze to hers, and nodded because speech was impossible. He was just like her. *I abandoned you the same way my mother abandoned me.*

Abby rubbed his back and laid her free hand on Emily's shoulder. "Your Dad--Mike--said some things when Seth came home after you were born that he shouldn't have."

Emily's pale face contorted into confusion. "What did he say?"

He said, "It doesn't matter what he said, sunshine. I stayed away, but I shouldn't have. Will you ever forgive me?"

Emily stared at him for a long time, her pain and grief playing over her blanched face before she ran from the room. The raw ache in his soul hadn't hurt this much since the night Abby had told him she didn't love him.

She called out Emily's name as the front door slammed.

She stood to run after her, but he caught her. "Let me, Abby."

"She's so mad at both of us."

"Yeah, she is. But it's me she's furious at. I can't lose her now that I found her. I just can't." He grabbed his jacket, left by the front door and stepped off the porch into the pouring rain.

He slid the barn door closed. His eyes quickly adjusted to the low glow of the single fluorescent light. Emily stood by her horse's stall. "I don't want to talk to you."

"I think I need to talk to you."

She looked over her shoulder at him.

His gut twisted into knots at her pain. He held her gaze. "I've always loved your mother, Emily. I still do. Some day I'd like for us to be a family."

She shook her head and turned back to the mare. "No. I already have a father."

He stepped closer and fisted his hands in his pockets. "I'm not asking you to stop thinking of Mike as your dad. I just want to be a part of your life too."

She tilted her head and shivered. Her damp t-shirt was much too thin for the chill of the day. He took off his jacket and set it across her shoulders. She looked up at him with big green eyes so much like his own, his breath caught. He studied her face. The shape of her chin was his. The way her lips pulled downward at one corner when she was bemused mirrored him.

"Maybe you're a little too late."

Her bitter words bored into him and settled in his chest. He turned to leave the barn.

"Your dad. He knew...about me, didn't he?"

Turning to face her, he sucked in a breath of the damp air, heavy with the scents of the horses and sweet hay. "Yeah. You stand to inherit a lot of his money when you turn eighteen. And from me too."

Emily widened her eyes at him.

He shook his head and stared at the hay-littered floor. "Emily, I know you may not believe this. But I've always loved you even though I didn't know you."

He turned and escaped into the dismal gray day, glad the rain mixed with the bitter tears he could no longer hold in.

* * * *

Abby stopped pacing the moment the front door opened.

"I want to go to Dad's."

She rushed over to the doorway of the living room. "You're drenched."

Emily shook with cold and the force of her tears. Abby lifted Seth's leather jacket from her shoulders and brushed her damp hair from her forehead. Emily jerked away from her touch.

She fisted her hand. "Oh, sugarbaby, I never wanted to hurt you."

"I'm calling Dad. I can't stay here."

"Emily." She waited until her daughter stopped. Emily squared her shoulders and turned. "There's something about your dad you should know."

Emily folded her arms and shifted her head in impatient defiance. "Why should I believe you?"

"Because I've never lied to you about anything else...ever."

"Well, I think this one lie makes up for all the ones you didn't tell, don't you?" Emily turned away.

"I've wanted to tell you about Seth since he came home, but Mike wouldn't let me. He's even threatened me."

"What do you mean?"

Abby leaned against the doorframe of the living room and sagged. "He told me he'd go to a tabloid. Mike married me for my money, sugarbaby. He and Tammy Jo have been together forever, but after she went to college, he asked me to marry him. I was pregnant with you. He devised the plan that we'd fool people into thinking you were his."

Emily hiccoughed and tilted her head to meet her eyes. "Seth said he's always loved me, but why didn't he ever come see me?"

She swallowed hard. It was time to tell her the whole truth. "When you were little, I wanted you to know about Seth, even if he wasn't in your life. Mike wouldn't hear of it. Over the years, he made me believe Seth abandoned you."

She puckered her brow. "How?"

"By lying to me. He never told me what he'd told Seth when he came to see you after you were born. What Mike said hurt Seth and made him believe you'd be better off never knowing him. Mike then told me Seth wanted nothing to do with his Indian bastard."

Emily jerked and stared at her. "Why would Daddy say those terrible things?"

"Because he's hiding something himself. He doesn't want Tammy Jo to know the truth, is my guess." She stepped forward and caressed the tears from her daughter's cheeks. "I think he lied to her the same way he's lied to everyone else. Including you, baby."

"What do you mean?" Emily's voice cracked.

She dragged Emily into her arms and held onto her as tightly as she dared. "By his treachery, he's robbed you of ever knowing your real father. He never wanted you to know Seth. And he wouldn't have kept me away from the only man I've ever loved."

* * * *

Abby paced the kitchen while Seth wore out the floor of the living room. She glanced at the clock on the stove again. Carolann and Frank were due any minute. Emily had all but begged to stay home from school, but Abby had insisted she go.

She didn't want her daughter to see how her grandparents reacted when they found out the truth.

"They're here." Seth's baritone jarred her to a stop, and she sucked in a breath.

Carolann knocked on the kitchen door as she opened it. "Hey, we got here as soon as we could."

The woman who'd become a mother to her after hers died rushed over and wrapped her in a surprisingly strong hug, considering her petite stature.

Abby hugged her back and choked on her heart. "Hi, Mom."

Frank entered the kitchen and closed the door.

"Dad."

Frank kissed Abby on the forehead.

Carolann noticed Seth standing in the doorway between the dining area and the living room. "Seth. What the heck are you doing here?" There was no mistaking the smile in Carolann's voice as she hugged him.

As he shook Frank's hand, the judge asked, "What's going on?"

Abby met Seth's gaze. "Let's go into the living room. Seth and I have something to tell you.

Carolann and Frank sat on the couch clasping each other's hands while Abby and Seth told them about Emily. By the end of the confession, Carolann and she were crying and Frank stared at her as if he didn't ever want to see her again.

Maybe he didn't.

Frank had never liked her mother. He'd blamed her for dragging the reputation of his friend into the mud. He'd never made Abby feel unwelcome, but she knew he'd considered her father nuts for throwing away everything and marrying an Indian whore.

"Does Mike know?"

Seth stood behind Abby's chair--the same chair Emily had sat in yesterday. His hand rested on her shoulder, tightened ever so slightly, trying to give comfort even though there possibly couldn't be any as he answered Frank. "Yes, Mike knows. He knew Abby was pregnant with my baby when he talked her into marrying him."

Carolann wiped at her tears and squared her shoulders. Abby hated the paleness of the older woman's face. The grief and betrayal made her look ten years older than her sixty-five years. Abby immediately thought about her tenuous heart condition when Carolann squeezed her hand into a fist over her left breast.

Carolann shook her head. "Why would Mike talk you into marrying..."

"I think I know why." Frank leaned over his long legs and scrubbed his face in his convulsing hands before looking at Abby. "Mike never got a loan, did he?"

"I don't know what you're asking." She sucked in a deep breath and looked at their pain-stricken faces.

Frank narrowed his eyes. "Mike told us he applied for a loan after we signed the Circle R over to him in hopes to save it from the bank and the tax collectors. When I asked him what collateral he had, he said he borrowed against Crawford Creek at your insistence. I thought it was odd at the time. That greedy bast--James McAllister hated my guts ever since I put his younger brother in the state pen for arson and insurance fraud back when I was the DA." He gritted his teeth as he referred to Tammy Jo's father, who had been the bank president fifteen years ago.

Frank let out a long sigh. "McAllister calling in the mortgage got us in the predicament we were in, in the first place. I couldn't believe he'd give my boy a loan. Unless he was just thankful Mike was no longer chasing his daughter's skirt."

"He never borrowed money from a bank." Seth's hard voice added to the tension in the stuffy room. "He never borrowed the money, period."

"Dear God, how much did he take from you?" Carolann covered her heart.

Before she could reassure the woman she loved as a second mother, Seth replied, "Almost everything. He may be a decent father to my daughter, but he's a lousy friend."

* * * *

Abby turned the corner and stopped dead. In the parking lot of the nursing home, Mike leaned against her Silverado. His hands were in the pockets of his bronze-colored pants, and his hat shaded his face. His Sheriff's Department Tahoe parked beside her truck. He looked over at her and removed his mirrored sunglasses.

As she adjusted the strap of her oversized purse, she headed toward him and tried to ignore the rapid pounding of her heart. No doubt by the scowl, Emily or his parents had talked to him.

But she'd bet it was Emily. She'd been in a major funk since Sunday. Abby stayed out of her way, but made it known she was willing to talk when Emily was ready. Obviously, she'd chosen to talk to Mike.

"Hey." She stopped in front of him and looked around, wishing they weren't in such a public place. Other nurses and staff were leaving at the end of the afternoon shift, and she hated the curious stares.

Mike didn't seem in a hurry to look at her. He pushed away from the side of the truck and glanced to the side before meeting her eyes. The cold turbulence she saw in the dark depths caused her to gasp.

She swallowed hard, but the lump in her throat didn't move. "I was going to call you."

His jaw worked as if he was releasing his back teeth. "My distraught daughter beat you to it. I hope you enjoyed hurting her."

"She deserves to know."

He glanced away and shrugged. "I told her I knew nothing about you being pregnant with Seth's baby. Nice little performance with my parents too, by the way. But when it came to your crying that I married you for your money and my shock that you'd lie to me, who do you think they believed? You or me?"

The parking lot shifted under her feet and opened up, and she pitched into a bottomless pit. She hugged herself, hoping the world soon righted itself. "Why are you doing this? You were my best friend. I loved you. No, I never was in love with you, but we had ten good years together." Not to mention a childhood before then.

He took a step toward her and scowled. "I raised your brat, Abby. I even loved her. But what thanks do I get for my sacrifice? The first time that son-of-a-bitch shows back up, you can't wait to fall into bed with him and destroy what's mine. Do you know what I stand to lose if your version of the truth becomes public knowledge?"

She wanted to back up, but she called on her pride and stayed her ground, though it wobbled dangerously under her feet. "I have a guess. Tammy Jo."

He bore down on her like a lion stalking a deer and leaned closer. "I lose every fucking thing I gave up for you. And I'll be damned if I'll lose it again."

His low growl flattened her as surely as if the lion had pounced on the deer. She shook from the force of so many emotions colliding within her--fear, pain, anger and betrayal were just a few.

As he got into the cruiser, he put his sunglasses on. "And Abby, my version of your sins are about to become public knowledge. I just sold the story to *The National News* this morning. Hope you have a great day."

She closed her eyes against the burn. He'd sold his lie to the most notorious gossip rag out there. She would hold it together if it was the last thing she did. But the tears gushed over the dam of her determination. She opened her eyes and released the panic on a strangled breath.

Seth.

He was the only one who'd know how to counter this madness. She got into the truck and turned the ignition with a shaky hand. On the radio, his baritone sang out in unison with Amanda Lang's sultry voice,

"In the heat of night we'll forget the coldness of day.

Baby, we'll worry about tomorrow when it comes.

Oh, yeah, why don't you stay? Why don't you stay?"

She switched the radio off and backed out of the parking lot.

Chapter 12

"You really are a cowboy."

Seth tugged on the reins to bring the horse to a stop and turned in the saddle at the sound of the silky voice at the rail of the corral. Amanda smiled and pushed flyaway blond hair out of her face.

"I wasn't expecting you until tomorrow." He steered the gelding around and trotted across the corral to her.

She pouted her deep purple lips. "I'm happy to see you too, baby. I thought we could spend the day together."

He dismounted and patted the sorrel's neck. "Amanda, I'm seeing someone."

She laughed and put her hand on her hip, drawing his gaze down her body. Dressed in a short miniskirt, low-cut blouse and high heels, she had a body that graced fashion magazines and had both young and old men hyperventilating. Except him. He preferred Abby's soft curves to Amanda's workout sculpted, nearly non-existent muscles, made so from starvation diets and popping pills.

"Since when has that stopped you? You know... I've never had a roll in the hay. Care to oblige me?"

"No. I won't oblige you. This woman isn't like the rest." *She's not like you.*

He pushed his hat back on his forehead. The day was a warm one, and he'd spent the past several hours rounding up calves. The other cowboys were back at the bunkhouse. He planned to take care of his horse and join the boys for supper.

Straightening her back and squaring her shoulders, Amanda lost her Hollywood smile. "She's the one you've been hung up on since ARS, isn't she?"

"Amanda, let it alone."

"She is. I thought she was married and had a kid." She'd removed her sunglasses and looked at him through black fake lashes with pale green eyes.

"I have to take care of the horse. Come around to the entrance of the barn and we'll talk."

He led the horse into the barn, poured out a ration of oats and filled a trough with water. He removed the saddle and the bridle and laughed when she wrinkled her nose as she came through the door.

"Eww... They say LA stinks. I'll take the smog over country air any day."

"LA does stink." He set the saddle in the tack room and returned with a brush. He'd ridden hard, and the gelding deserved a rubdown before being put out to pasture.

"Yeah, but not like this." She covered her nose with a perfectly manicured hand. "Gawd!"

"And to think you wanted a roll in the hay. That's what you're smelling, by the way. Besides, the horses, the leather and me. I spent the day rounding up steers."

"I change my mind. What the hell do all those women find attractive about cowboys?"

Chuckling, he brushed the sorrel's red coat to a shine. He'd often wondered that himself.

She waved a hand in front of her nose, then cocked a delicate eyebrow and put her free hand on her nearly non-existent hip. "So, tell me about this woman."

"You aren't going to let this alone, are you?"

"You know me better than that."

He paused in his work and looked across the horse's back at her. "Yes, she's the one."

"I take it she's no longer married, but what about the kid? Thought you didn't want any."

I didn't want any with you. He sighed and remembered that particularly sticky conversation from seven years ago. He and Amanda were going at it hot and heavy, and she was getting a little bit too attached. After one bout of wild sex, she'd asked him if he'd ever considered settling down and having kids. He'd told her a flat out *no.* The next day, he left her bed and made sure she heard he was seeing someone else less than a week later.

He set the brush down and led the horse from the barn. When he turned to her, she had her arms crossed and tapped the toe of her sky-high hooker shoe. Rubbing his hand over the back of his neck, he said, "I didn't raise the one I had. So, I figured it was foolish to want more."

Her foot stopped moving mid-tap, and her perfectly arched brows drew together, until his meaning dawned on her. Then her mouth fell open, and she dropped her arms to her side. "You have a kid?"

He glanced away. "Yeah. You'll meet her Saturday. Great little singer and not a bad songwriter."

"How old is she?"

"Fourteen." He met her rounded eyes. The fake lashes looked even more ridiculous. "Her mother is the woman."

"Wait. That would mean..." He could almost see her doing the math in her head. "She was pregnant when you were on ARS, wasn't she?"

Her tone said everything. Amanda and he had become friends during the show, and after he discovered Abby had married Mike, they'd become lovers.

But all that didn't change the fact, they'd also been competitive rivals who'd wanted to be the winner of the first *America's Rising Star*. And Seth, with his hard luck story of his mother dying young and his father's estrangement, had won the sympathy vote. He'd been one of only two country singers on the show and the only one to advance to the final rounds. Not that he couldn't sing, but who knew if he'd have won if not for those votes?

And he would have definitely lost if the world had known he'd knocked up his seventeen-year-old girlfriend. Technically, he'd broken the law since he'd been eighteen and she a minor. Even if he'd married her, that wouldn't have changed the fact she'd been only a senior in high school.

Damn, maybe Abby had been right.

Her coming with him would have ruined his chance.

"Yeah, Abby was, and I was a fool to ever leave her."

She smiled and closed the space between them. "You obviously love her. I'm happy for you, Seth."

And then she kissed him square on the lips.

* * * *

Abby stared at the cherry red BMW convertible as she stopped her truck beside it in the driveway. She got out and looked around. The sounds of earthmoving equipment came from the back of the house. Horses munched on grass in the pasture beside the barn.

"...you, Seth."

She whipped her head around at the sound of the husky female voice.

What the hell? She headed in the direction of the door and stopped dead a few feet in from the opening. Her heart splintering apart at the sight of the tall, leggy blonde in Seth's arms.

He stepped away from the pop star as if burned, or rather caught. "Abby."

She wanted to run, but forced her feet to stay put.

The pain ripping through her chest was totally new. She'd never felt like this around Tammy Jo, even when she'd figured out Mike had been cheating with her for years.

But then, she'd never loved Mike.

The blonde turned around and looked her up and down.

Abby felt especially frumpy in the apple green scrub pants and ladybug themed smock when compared to the designer clothes barely covering the supermodel body.

Amanda stepped forward and held out a hand that was as perfect as the rest of her. "It's nice to meet you, Abby. I'm Amanda."

Had he told his girlfriend about her? She forced her hand to shake the softest hand she'd ever touched. *Well, it's not nice to meet you.* "Uh... yeah."

Seth came to her and put his arm around her shoulders. From the look in his eyes, he knew he'd been caught. Oh, God, how could she have been so stupid? A man like him would never settle for her. He'd played her perfectly. All he'd ever wanted was Emily.

Now that she knew he was her father, he'd move on.

Amanda slipped on her fancy sunglasses and smiled at him. "See you tomorrow."

He only nodded. Once Amanda walked past and her car door closed, Abby turned on him. "How dare you lead me on?"

She didn't wait for his lie and rushed from the barn.

He caught her arm as she was about to open her truck door and swung her around. Damn it, she was bawling again.

With his fingers, he brushed at her tears. "I didn't lead you on."

She jerked away from him. "Then what is she doing here?"

"We're going to sing together at the concert Saturday and film a video for the song we did together."

"You gonna sleep with her too?"

"No!" He grabbed her upper arms and stared into her eyes. "Damn it! I love you. I only want you."

She pulled away from him again, yanked open the truck door and threw herself into the rig. As she cranked the engine, she glared out the open window. "Then why the hell were you kissing her?"

When he didn't answer, she shifted into gear and put the pedal almost to the floorboards. She had a sick sense of satisfaction when gravel sprayed up to smack him as she sped away.

* * * *

"Fuck!" He wiped his hat off and beat his thigh with it. He should have told Abby about inviting Amanda to McAllister. But her thinking the worst wasn't his fault. Abby should trust him.

"Hey, Seth, you comin'?" Tucker Cowley called from the direction of the bunkhouse.

He slammed the hat on his head and brushed at the dust on his jeans. His shins stung where the pebbles had hit him. "Yeah. I'm coming."

His long strides ate up the distance, and as he got closer, Tucker asked, "Who was the blonde?"

"Amanda Lang."

"Wow." Tucker turned and walked beside him. "Is she the reason Abby tore out of here like a bat out of hell? Let me guess. Woman trouble?"

He narrowed his eyes on the ranch manager.

Tucker snickered and cuffed him on the shoulder. "Join the club. My girl walked out on me two days ago. Hey, wanna go to Gatlin's later?"

"Yeah, I could use a good drunk about right now."

* * * *

For the first hour of the ride through the pastures of the Double K Thursday afternoon, neither Seth nor Emily spoke. She'd met him at the house after calling to say she needed to talk to him.

When they'd stopped by the hunting cabin, they dismounted to let the horses drink and nibble on the grass on the bank of the stream. The late afternoon sun slanted through the ponderosa pines and the hackberry trees to dabble shade over the water.

Emily ambled to the bank and sat on a moss-covered rock. She tossed stones into the creek and looked around. "Is it true?"

He lifted his hat off his head and ran the back of his hand over his forehead, more in frustration than to wipe off the sweat that collected there. Crouching beside her, he plowed his hand through his hair. He looked out over the water wishing he had remembered to grab some magic potion that would make the pain in her voice and eyes go away.

He returned his hat to his head and glanced at Emily. The light filtering through the trees set the hair falling over her back on fire and painted her in an ethereal glow. He swallowed hard and cleared his throat, but his voice still sounded gruff when he finally spoke. "What's true?"

"Daddy said he didn't know about me...about you being my...you know."

What the hell was she talking about? "Emily, what did Mike say to you?"

When she spoke, she didn't look at him. "I called him Monday night. I had to know if he...if he still wanted me around. Mom told me about some horrible things he supposedly said and did, and I had to hear it from him." Her face pinched with the effort to get the difficult words out. "He was shocked. He got really mad and yelled at me that he didn't know. And that whatever you and Mom said about him knowing was a lie."

He fisted his hands and clamped his jaw down so hard his teeth hurt. "He's lying, sunshine," he gritted out when he could speak. "He knew your mother was pregnant with you and that I'm your father."

She turned to him and narrowed her watery eyes. "But why would he lie?"

"I think he's protecting himself. He's afraid if the truth comes out he'll lose something. Maybe he lied to Tammy Jo. I don't know."

"Mom said the same thing the other night. About him lying to Tammy Jo."

He sucked in a breath and forced himself to calm his rage. "But trust me. He knew about you, then lied to keep me away. He's the one who convinced your momma to keep me a secret from you. He never wanted you to know I'm your father."

She shook her head. "That's what Mom said too. None of this makes sense. I feel like my whole life has been one gigantic lie. I don't know what to believe anymore." She stood and went over to where her mare munched on the tender grass under a tree. "I don't know who I am anymore." The mare gave her head a shake and nickered as Emily stroked her neck. "Momma keeps apologizing, but that doesn't change the fact I'm not really Emily Ritter." She leaned her head against the thoroughbred's neck, knocking her hat onto the ground where it lay forgotten. "But I'm not Emily Kendall either."

He was at her side in a heartbeat and laid a hand on her quivering shoulder. "Maybe you're a little of both."

She lifted her head and looked over her shoulder at him. The sight of her red-rimmed eyes clenched his heart. "Momma said she's afraid of some kind of newspaper article. Do you know anything about that?"

"No." But he could guess. Mike's threats. He'd have to call Gary to start doing some damage control. Flicking away the tears on her cheeks with a thumb, he rummaged up a smile that threatened to slip off his face. "We'd better start back."

She swallowed again and murmured, "Okay. You coming over to our place tonight?"

"I don't think so."

She wrinkled her brow. "You and Momma have a fight or something?"

"Your mom's mad at me. And I'm a little upset with her right now." His voice dipped low as he dragged it from some deep and hollow well inside his chest.

"You aren't leaving, are you?"

He stroked her soft cheek. "No, I'm not leaving."

"Good. I want to get to know you."

He closed his eyes for a beat. Dear God, her words healed the rip in his heart.

"I'm meeting with my band to go over some of the music I want to play on Saturday. Would you like to hang out with us if your mom says it's okay?"

"You bet!" She smiled and filled his chest with its brightness. Then she turned and wrapped her arms around him.

* * * *

Abby pushed the head of the vacuum over the old rug in the living room. Seth hadn't called, and after she'd almost called him, she'd hauled out the sweeper and started cleaning.

She'd heard about the camera crew shooting scenes for Seth's and Amanda Lang's video all over town. She'd also heard about his drunken antics at Gatlin's Tuesday night.

If he hadn't been guilty of wanting the blond bimbo, he would have come to Abby, not gone out with the Cowley brothers to paint the town red. Wouldn't he?

Maybe she should call him.

No. Damn it, she wasn't the one caught kissing someone else. She viciously pushed the head one more time over the rug.

The doorbell rang, and she turned off the vacuum cleaner. She opened the door and swayed a little. What the hell was Tammy Jo doing at her door?

"Hello, Abby." Her hazel eyes flashed.

"Tammy Jo, what a surprise." *Surprise* didn't even touch what she was feeling.

Tammy Jo looked past her into the entry. "May I come in? I need to speak with you."

She was tired of feeling like she was the one with the big scarlet A on her chest when she was with this woman.

She stepped back to let Tammy Jo step through the door, gesturing toward the living room. "Come on in."

Tammy Jo looked around and rubbed her hand over her extended belly. "This is nice."

She about fell over. Tammy Jo was offering her a compliment? "Thanks. Can I get you anything?"

"No, thank you." Tammy Jo moved around the room, looking at the photos hanging on the walls. Most of them were of Emily and her parents. "You know we all must have been blind. She looks so much like Seth."

The earth swayed under her again. What was she up to? "What's this about, Tammy Jo?"

She turned toward her. "Mike told me you lied and tricked him into marrying him."

She sat on the wingchair. Something about her tone had her asking, "But you don't believe him?"

Tammy Jo sat on the couch and continued to rub her belly. "I don't know what to believe, but I know he hasn't been completely honest with me lately."

She focused on Tammy Jo's pale face and the strain and dark circles she'd tried to cover with makeup and powder. "Are you feeling okay?"

"I'll be all right." She squinted as if fighting a wince. "Last month before John Kendall died, I hired a private eye to follow Mike and you."

"Why?"

"I thought you were having an affair." She smiled but it didn't quite reach her eyes.

"Mike and I are--were nothing but friends."

Tammy Jo nodded and rubbed her belly again. "I figured that out. But the PI found out some things about Mike that shocked me. He's been diverting money from my trust fund into a private account he has set up in Mexico. He also sold the story about you tricking him and having Seth's baby to the tabloids and received a substantial payout. That, too, went into his secret account." She paused and looked down at the floor. "But the worst thing the PI discovered is Mike may be involved with some kind of illegal dealings. He might be transporting illegal aliens over the Mexican border."

Dear God! She wanted to ask her more about Mike's actions, but Tammy Jo was distraught enough. "I'm sorry. I can ease your mind about the article because it isn't true. Mike threatened me he'd sell the lie that I'd tricked him into marrying him if Seth and I told Emily the truth about him being her father."

How could Mike do this to her--to Emily--to his wife?

Tammy Jo took a deep breath. This time she couldn't hide the wince. "So, he's always known?"

"Yes. Mike married me for my money to save the Circle R."

"He never used your money for the R. He set up his illegal ring. That's how he saved the ranch."

Her heart twisted and her gut clenched. "What?"

The other woman looked away. "I'm sorry, Abby, that's all I really know. Did Seth know about the baby?"

She took a deep breath, folded her hands into a tight knot in her lap. "Yes, he knew before the talent show, and I planned to wait for Seth to come home. But I was so afraid of what people would say about me when they found out I was pregnant. I didn't tell anyone except Mike."

She told Tammy Jo everything--about Mike's lies and betrayals. And her reasons for not going with Seth.

Tammy Jo's face became paler, and she fisted her hand over her swollen belly. "He lied to me." She sniffed and seemed to melt. Her eyes glistened, but she covered the pain with anger. She stood, rubbed her back and paced in front of the windows, her low heels clipping sharply on the floor. "I hated Harvard. But Daddy insisted I major in business and finance and forget my dreams of being a model. I was there a month, and I'd call Mike every night. God, I loved him. But Daddy hated him."

She paused and picked up a wooden frame containing a photo of Mike and Emily together when she was a toddler. "So, I devised a plan for us to run away. I began drawing money from the account Daddy set up for me and transferring it into one I'd opened. He called me about the money and told me he'd cut me off if I was planning something with Mike." She stopped and met her eyes. "I didn't care. I'd been already offered a modeling job." As if fighting a war with her emotions, Tammy Jo blinked and sniffed. "I called Mike with my plan. I'd send him a plane ticket to New York and meet him there."

Abby didn't like the way Tammy Jo looked. Lines of both emotional and physical pain riddled her stunning face. She stood and went over to Tammy Jo. "You need to sit down."

Tammy Jo didn't fight her as she helped her onto the couch. Abby took her wrist and felt for a pulse. As she concentrated on the too-fast heartbeat, Tammy Jo went on with her story. "He broke down and told me that you'd seduced him and were pregnant, and he planned to marry you." She shook her head, the first of her tears flowing in big drops down her smooth cheeks. "You never seduced him, did you?"

She let go of Tammy Jo's hand and laid her hands over the swell of her belly. If her suspicions were correct, she should be able to feel the next contraction as a subtle jerking of the muscles beneath the surface. "No, I never seduced Mike or anyone else. I've always known he loved you, and he's always known I loved Seth. He told me you and he broke up, and that he hated to see me alone. At the same time, rumors of Seth seeing Amanda Lang surfaced, and I freaked, I guess. I agreed to Mike's idiotic plan and married him."

Tammy Jo's belly jerked under her hands. Tammy Jo winced and laid her hands over hers.

"How long have you been having pains?"

Tammy Jo's eyes widened and her breathing came in quick spurts. "I've had Braxton Hicks contractions for weeks, but this is different."

"How long have the pains been different?"

"Since last night. I thought it was just the stress of everything going on right now." Then fear mingled with the pain in her wide eyes. "God, it's too early to be in labor. I'm not due for another three weeks."

"Yeah, well, I don't think this guy's gonna wait that long." She felt the beginning of the next contraction as the muscles under Tammy Jo's skirt hardened, and it was stronger than the last one.

Tammy Jo cried out as it hit the peak. Sweet Jesus, she was in full-fledged labor.

"I should call Mike." Tammy Jo gasped at the end and reached for her handbag, but Abby beat her to it and handed the expensive leather purse to her. "Thank you." Tammy Jo called her husband. He wasn't answering his cell, so she left a message. She hung up and dropped the smart phone back into her bag. "I don't know where he is. He's supposed to be at the fairgrounds overseeing the carnival rides people. Ahh! God!"

Tammy Jo arched her back with the pain, a dark wet stain spreading on her skirt.

Abby jumped into action, grabbed Tammy Jo's shoulders and helped her lie on the couch.

"What's happening?"

"Your water just broke. You need to remember to breathe through the contractions. It'll help with the pain. I'm going to get some towels and call 9-1-1. I'll be right back. Okay? Who's your doctor?"

"Dr. Richard Mason in Amarillo." Tammy Jo's eyes were wide as she looked down at the wet gush staining her skirt, the couch, and the floor. "Oh, God. Hurry. I'm scared."

Abby squeezed the woman's shoulder. Scared? She was petrified. An ambulance was at least twenty minutes away, and the hospital Tammy Jo was probably hoping to deliver in was an hour away. She prayed she could get Tammy Jo out of her living room before the baby came.

Tammy Jo screamed, and she realized she wasn't moving and kicked it into gear. She called the ambulance, ran to her bedroom, grabbed a bunch of towels and a sheet, then her stethoscope and a blood pressure cuff she had shoved in the back of the bathroom closet. She washed her hands and threw a bottle of alcohol and a pair of scissors into the laundry basket in which she'd tossed everything else. Then she looked around for something to clamp the umbilical cord with. She found a ponytail band on the windowsill and grabbed. Praying the elastic would do the trick and that the alcohol would sterilize everything, she ran out of the bedroom.

"Oh, God! The pains are coming too fast." Tammy Jo thrashed on the couch as she entered the room.

"Breathe through it, Tammy." She set the basket down, knelt beside the couch, slipped the blood pressure cuff around her arm and took the reading.

As she removed the stethoscope buds from her ears, she said, "The ambulance is on the way, but I have a feeling we don't have that much time."

Tammy Jo shook her head and tears ran down her face, taking what little makeup she wore with it. "No, oh, God, no."

"Tammy Jo, listen to me." She removed the blood pressure cuff and took her hand. When she sobbed again, Abby squeezed her hand and repeated her command. "No, listen to me."

Tammy Jo looked at her.

"Remember, I'm a nurse. It's been a while since I've worked labor and delivery, but we can do this."

Slowly, Tammy Jo nodded, and Abby smiled. "Good. Now, here's what I need to do. I'm going to check to see what's going on down there. Is that okay?"

Another contraction hit, and Tammy Jo screamed again but this time she tried to breathe through it. Abby listened with the stethoscope at her belly for the baby's heartbeat. She breathed out a long sigh of relief when the gentle beating came to her strong and steady.

When the contraction was over, Tammy Jo met her gaze and licked her dry lips. "Help me, Abby. Please, don't let my baby die."

She pushed back Tammy Jo's damp hair from her forehead. "Let's do this."

She discovered Tammy Jo was fully dilated and the baby was ready to crown, then covered her with the sheet. Tammy Jo's contractions went from coming every one and a half minutes to coming every thirty seconds. Like it or not, Baby Ritter was being born right here on her couch, and she was the only one to help him into the world.

Talk about freaking cosmic irony.

Tammy Jo suffered through another contraction.

"Tammy Jo, I need you to listen to me and things will go better for all three of us."

Tammy Jo nodded and stared up at her, wide eyes made glossy with her pain and fear.

"The ambulance is at least another fifteen minutes away. They were on another run when I called in. But we can do this. From the looks of it, he's ready to meet his momma and is in a damned big hurry to do so. I can bring him to the world, but you need to help me, understand?"

Another contraction hit and she screamed, "I just want him to be okay!"

She moved down to kneel next to Tammy Jo's legs, laying out a bunch of the clean towels between her thighs. "He will be great. His heartbeat is strong and your blood pressure is a little high, but not unusually so. On the next contraction, I want you to push as hard as you can. Got it?"

"No, can't we wait?" She thrashed her head from side to side as another contraction came on strong and nature took over.

"Push! Tammy, push!" She put her stethoscope buds in her ears and laid the drum on Tammy Jo's belly. The baby's heart rate was faint but steady.

When the next contraction started, Abby didn't even have to tell her to push. Tammy Jo screamed her way through the pain and bore down as hard as she could. Abby quickly poured the alcohol over the scissors and the ponytail band and laid them on a towel to dry. With the next push, the baby's head fully crowned. She laughed at the sight of the dark hair. "That's it, Tammy. Push!"

With the next pain, Tammy Jo delivered her son with one gigantic push. Abby caught the baby and immediately used a towel and her fingers to clean his face, mouth, and nose.

He instantly let out a howl to fill his lungs with air.

Tammy Jo moaned the same time the siren of the ambulance squealed in the distance.

"Let me see my baby." Her voice was raw from screaming and weak from her ordeal. But it was full of awe.

Abby laid the squirming, crying baby on his mommy's belly. Using the elastic band, she crudely clamped the umbilical cord then cut it with the scissors and wrapped him up in a fresh towel. She'd let the hospital make the final ties to the cord.

"God, he's beautiful, Tammy Jo. He's absolutely beautiful." She held him and felt the sting of tears as they ran from her eyes.

She placed him in Tammy Jo's open arms, and the woman stared at him with unadulterated love.

The doorbell rang, and Abby scrambled up onto her feet and wavered a little until she got her legs under her. Tammy Jo wasn't the only one weak from the strain. She let in the EMTs and almost hugged the first one across her threshold. "Thank God you're here." She ushered them into the living room and started spouting off vitals and times.

One of the medics looked at Abby. "You delivered the baby."

Tammy Jo smiled. "Yes, she did. I don't know what I would've done without her."

Abby patted Tammy Jo on her arm as the medics readied the gurney to transfer mother and baby onto it. "You did all the hard work. I have to say, you did a fine job of it."

Tammy Jo grinned from ear to ear.

The men moved her from the blood-covered couch to the clean white sheet on the gurney. Tammy Jo reached out and took her hand. "I won't let him destroy you, Abby. Thank you."

She squeezed her clammy fingers. "No, thank you for believing me. But I'm sorry too."

Once the ambulance left with Tammy Jo and her baby, she flopped onto the floor and looked at the bloody, wet mess of the couch and bath towels. Just like her life, everything was ruined.

Mike turned out to be a stranger, and Seth broke her heart.

But did he? She blinked as her mind raced with a new realization. If Seth was sleeping with Amanda Lang, why would he have spent the night raising hell at Gatlin's with Tucker and Vince Cowley, and why would he still be staying with Johanna?

When her gaze fell on the old sweeper, she broke down and laughed as tears ran down her cheeks. Just like her living room, maybe her life could be cleaned up too.

Chapter 13

Seth paced the bedroom of his bus. The band had come out on it. Damn, what was wrong with him? He slapped his thigh and stopped to peer at his reflection in the mirror. He and Amanda had spent the morning rehearsing their performance. Onstage now was the local band Lawman and they were working a crowd of about ten thousand.

The fair committee hadn't advertised Seth's performance and tried to keep Amanda's appearance quiet as he'd requested, but once she and the camera crew arrived, the game was up.

Then the paparazzi showed up after Mike sold his shitload of lies to a rag. He hoped Abby was holding up through everything. The news of her delivering Tammy Jo's baby yesterday was all over town.

So was Tammy Jo's refusal to see her husband.

Abby. He needed to talk to her. Staying angry with her for not trusting him was not worth the heartache. But she had to understand, he would always have professional relationships with women that required more contact than sharing office gossip around the water cooler. Potentially acting out sexy scenes with actresses in his videos, possibly singing love songs with other female singers, and God only knew what the crazy groupies would try to get to him. But Abby had to trust him enough to know his days of being a playboy were over. He only wanted her.

He wanted to come home to her and their daughter.

The ring in his jeans pocket felt heavy. It belonged on the hand of the woman he loved. He had no idea when he'd pop the question, but he wanted to do it soon.

The director of the video ducked her head through the doorway. "You're on in five minutes."

"Thanks." He grabbed his hat and guitar.

At the back of the stage, he took a deep breath and let it out slowly. Live video shoots were always nerve-wracking, but tonight he was out of sorts with his thoughts. He also had the added stress of knowing his daughter would perform with him later.

"Man, you okay?"

He nodded at the stagehand and adjusted his guitar. He took the wireless microphone as Amanda stepped up beside him.

He slipped the mic on and raised an eyebrow at her. "Who're you channeling?"

She shrugged and fluffed her hair. "Daisy Duke." She put her hands up and did a little twirl, showing off short denim shorts and a sleeveless plaid shirt tied below her breasts. She'd obviously forgone the buttons altogether, because her cleavage showed down to the knot. "What do you think?"

He laughed and pointed to the stilts pretending to be boots. "Don't break your neck."

She smiled and adjusted her mic. "Try to keep up."

"Right." Then he headed out onstage to the applauding hometown crowd. He waved and looked for Abby as he gave it all to a song he really was starting to hate.

Especially when he didn't see the woman he loved amongst the sea of excited faces.

* * * *

Abby stared at the massive silver signature of Seth Kendall on the side of the shiny black tour bus. The tail of the last *L* scrolled and formed an outline of a guitar.

Emily unlocked the door and turned. "You coming?"

"Are you sure about this?"

Emily bounded up the steps and looked over her shoulder. "Yes. Seth told me to meet him here." She held up the key. "Why do you think he gave me this? After he's done with his set, he'll come get me while Amanda sings." Emily shuddered as Seth's voice faded and the crowd's cheer went up loud enough to be heard for miles around. "Holy crap, how many people do you think are out there?"

Abby glanced over the back of the outdoor stage. "Your grandma told me they sold over ten thousand tickets. About three times as many they normally do."

Emily paled and swayed a little on the top step.

"You gonna be okay?" She went up the steps and set her hand on Emily's shoulder.

She swallowed and met her gaze with widened eyes. "I don't know if I can do this, Momma. What if I get out there and freeze up?"

Abby smiled and turned Emily around. She had no choice but move into the bus. She followed and sucked in a breath when she got a look at the red and tan leather seating, the gray marble of the kitchenette and the polish of the finely grained, blond wood paneling.

Two guitars hung on the wall over the couch and a banjo leaned against the wall. She shook herself when she realized Emily was completely at home on the tour bus, setting her guitar case on the floor and flopping on the couch with her feet on the cushion. "Momma, did you hear me?"

"You'll be perfectly fine out there." She moved Emily's feet to the floor and sat beside her.

"How can you be so sure?"

She smoothed Emily's hair and smiled. "Because you have too much of your father in you to not feel right at home on a stage, whether you're singing to a handful of people or ten thousand."

Emily seemed to search her gaze for a long moment before looking away. "Momma, I'd really like to make a record. Seth said he'd help me and produce it. We could do it after his recording studio is finished on the Double K."

"I think that's a great idea." She couldn't believe she was agreeing to such a thing. For years, she'd tried to smother Emily's talent.

Emily sat straighter and stared at her. "Really?"

She wrapped her arm around her shoulders. "Yeah, really. I think it's great that you and Seth have music in common."

The smile melted, and Emily shrank in her embrace. "But Daddy won't allow it. He hates that I want to be a singer. All he talks about is me going to college."

"Emily, I'd like you to follow your dreams. But I think we need to talk about Mike."

"What about him?"

She considered her response. Now wasn't the time to spring what she knew on her, but when the time was right, she was going to suggest she agree not to spend so much time with Mike. "We'll talk after the show. Okay?"

Emily nodded and sighed as she glanced at a clock on the wall. "It's almost time." Opening her guitar case, she lifted the amplified acoustic out and set the strap around her shoulder.

Abby felt an overwhelming sense of love and peace. Her little girl had grown into a beautiful young woman.

The door opened and Seth stepped into the bus. He stopped short when he saw her. She stood and smiled. "Hi."

"Hi." He took a step toward her and paused again. "I...I was looking for you in the crowd. I almost fell over an amplifier cord because I wasn't paying attention."

This thrilled her more than anything he could have said to her. She put the knuckles of her fisted hand to her mouth to keep from laughing. "That would have made an interesting video."

"To say the least."

She wanted to kiss the grin right off his handsome face.

"Oh, for God's sake." Emily raised her hands in exasperation. "Will you two kiss and make up already?"

Abby couldn't hold in the laugh any longer. She took a step toward Seth the same time he moved toward her. His low chuckle filled her heart as he pulled her into his arms. Feathering his fingers over her cheek, he gazed into her eyes. She'd never doubt his love again. "You silly woman. I've loved you since I was six years old and you told me to go jump in a lake after I said you looked like a sissy in that frilly pink dress you wore to my birthday party."

She wrapped her arms around him as the sting started in her sinuses. Damn, she was going to start crying. "And I've loved you ever since you stood up to those bullies on the playground when they started calling me names."

"Which time was that?"

"Every time." Then she kissed him.

He wrapped her up and deepened the healing until Emily reminded them they were not alone. "Okay, guys. I said kiss and make up, not make out."

Seth pulled back and set his forehead on hers. "But you have to trust me. I'll never betray you, but I do have a job and it requires playing nice to women like Amanda."

"I know. I don't have to like it. But I understand."

He kissed her quickly on the nose and pulled back. "I heard you were a real hero yesterday."

"All in the line of duty." She shrugged and felt her cheeks warm. "Tammy Jo will be okay. But Mike's really hurt her too."

Seth raised his brow.

"I'll tell you later."

Emily stepped between them, and Abby was surprised to see tears in her daughter's eyes as she wrapped her arms around her and Seth. "Now that we're all good, the old man and I have thousands of fans to entertain."

Seth tugged on Emily's ponytail. "Who are you calling old?"

She shrugged and stepped back. "If the shoe fits and all that."

* * * *

Seth stepped onto the stage and the crowd cheered. He glanced at Emily anxiously bouncing the toe of her boot on the wood floor in the wing then faced the audience. "Before I introduce my next duet partner, I'd like to thank all of you for coming out here tonight. Without y'all I wouldn't be here singing tonight." He paused as the crowd applauded and cheered. "But I paid a terrible personal price for my fame. One I've come to realize I'd have rather not paid."

He cleared his voice. The crowd settled down as they realized this wasn't a typical introduction, but a confession.

"Tonight I'd like to introduce you to someone who has recently come into my life, but there hasn't been a day I haven't thought of her in the past fifteen years." He looked back at Emily and held out his hand. "I'd like to present my daughter, Emily."

She stepped out and the crowd gave out a collective gasp. He waited until the chatter quieted down. He turned his mic off and whispered, "Ready?"

She nodded and took his hand. "Yeah. Let's do this."

He smiled, turned his mic on, and faced the band. "One...two...three."

As the band struck up the intro to the song he and Emily had written together, she stepped forward and belted out the first verse like a pro.

Dear God, she had the voice of an angel.

* * * *

"Holy crap, that was a rush!" Emily bounced down the stairs, heading for the tour bus. They'd sung four songs together then she'd finished with one of her own.

Seth wrapped his arm around her shoulder. "You were fantastic."

She looked up at him. Her smile rivaled the sun. "I talked to Mom about her letting me make a record. She said I could."

"Whoa. I thought we agreed to wait a little."

She stopped and faced him. "No, you agreed. I don't want to wait. I know I can do this, Seth. And with you endorsing me... C'mon. I'll be fifteen in a few months, and I'm far from the youngest singer ever to get her big break as a teenager. Loretta Lynn, Tanya Tucker, Leann Rhimes, Taylor Swift... I could go on."

"Yeah, and not one of them would tell you it's all a bed of roses. Emily, fame isn't all it's cracked up to be. I've done a lot of stupid things in the name of fame."

"I'm not you. Besides, you'd be there to help me." She stared up at him with eager green eyes that were surrounded with way too much makeup. He wanted his little girl, but he'd never have the little girl in the videos Abby had given to him. He did have this amazing young woman who was asking him to help her pursue her dreams.

He didn't need to read a parenting book about teenagers to know this was a rare event.

Or that he'd be a fool not to grab onto it with both hands. "Okay. We'll talk to your mom and maybe plan a trip to Nashville. I'll introduce you the president of my record company. If he likes what he hears, you'll get a deal."

"Oh God! Really?" She clasped her hands together and bounced on her toes in a tight little circle.

He held up a hand, stopping her when she faced him again. "But there're a few conditions in all this."

Some of her exuberance faded. "What conditions?"

"I produce at least your first three albums. I help you pick your music, and for the first four years, you only tour with me. You finish school and you must maintain at least a B plus average."

She caught her bottom lip between her teeth. "Okay. Anything else?"

"Yeah... I'd like you to add my name to yours."

"What do you mean?"

Seth stroked his goatee and cleared his throat. "You're my daughter, Emily. I'm planning to ask your mom to marry me. I'd like us to be a family and that includes you starting to think of me as your dad. I'd like to adopt you, just to make everything legal."

She turned away from him and wrapped her arms around her middle. "What about my dad--Mike?"

"Yeah, Seth, what about me?"

They both turned at the sound of Mike's voice as he stepped out of the shadows, pointing a gun at them.

"What are you doing?" As fear froze Seth's blood, he wrapped an arm around Emily's shoulders. She seemed to be too shocked to believe what was going on.

Mike was dressed casually in jeans and western shirt. He held a Glock with a steady hand. "I've lost everything because of this brat. So, I've decided to take some of it back."

"Daddy?" Emily's quiet voice shook with fear.

He jerked the gun toward her. "I gave up everything for you, Emily. I even loved you, but as soon as this son-of-a-bitch shows up, you fall all over him."

She sobbed and clung to Seth's side. He pushed her behind him.

"Mike, put the gun down."

"Or what? You'll sing me a song?" He took a few steps toward them. "Do you have any idea how long I've hated your guts?

The question stung more than he wanted it to.

"Do you remember that time we competed in the Tri-County Rodeo?"

He hadn't wanted to enter, but his father insisted, hoping he'd win and get the notice of the national circuit. He'd been a senior in high school, a decent roper, but never wanted or aspired to be a rodeo cowboy. Mike had entered the same rodeo, as had half the wannabe cowboys in the area. Although Seth competed, he'd hoped Mike would win. But in the end, Seth got the silver buckle. The buckle he still wore when on stage. "That was a long time ago."

"Do you know what your beating me cost me?" Mike was close enough, the whiskey and the sweat smells wafted over. But he held that damned gun in a deadly steady hand. And way too close to the girl he'd give his life to protect.

Was this what a father's love was like?

"Dad wouldn't let me try again. He said that was the last rodeo and it was time to get serious about my life. Hell, you didn't even want to ride. That's all I ever wanted to do. It was my ticket out of this hell-hole of a town."

Was he off his rocker? "Put the gun down and let's talk about this."

"Fuck you. I'm done talking." He reached for Emily, and before Seth could move, Mike had her by the arm and the gun pointed at the back of her skull.

Emily screamed and sobbed louder. Her distress cut through him in a way nothing ever had. "You don't want to do this. What about Tammy Jo and your new baby?"

"What about them? Tammy Jo betrayed me. She won't even let me see my boy."

None of this was making sense. "Mike, what's going on here? What are you going to do with Emily?"

He moved the gun from her head to train it on him. "A young girl who appears to be white? Do you have any idea how much I'll get for her on the market?"

The market? Did he seriously mean the human trafficking market?

Sara Walter Ellwood

"Put the gun down, Mike."

Deputy Clint Grier stood behind him with a Glock pointed at his boss's head. "You know I won't miss if I pull this trigger."

"Drop it, Ritter." Out of the darkness came another voice. Seth recognized it as the Texas Ranger, Wayne Cover. "We have enough to send your sorry ass up the river. Don't add murder to the list."

The part-time singer and fulltime sheriff's deputy moved in at the same time as the drummer Texas Ranger and the other sheriff's deputy from Grier's band.

Mike was completely surrounded and with nothing to lose, he was more dangerous than before. He shifted his aim at Emily again.

Seth didn't think his actions through. He let instinct take over and fell forward, taking Emily into his arms and falling to the ground.

A gun went off and everything went black as pain exploded through his right shoulder. The last thing he heard was Abby screaming his name and his little girl's sobs.

* * * *

Abby and Emily held onto each other in the hospital waiting room. An ambulance had rushed Seth to the biggest medical center in Amarillo. He had to survive this. He had to!

The scene of him falling with Emily and Mike shooting him wouldn't stop playing in her head. Hell, the images of coming upon Mike holding that gun to her baby's head about killed her. As much as it had destroyed her to not walk onto the scene, she'd pulled back and immediately called Clint's phone number. His amateur band was closing the show and had just finished the set.

Carolann and Frank held each other across the aisle. No one spoke. The Texas Rangers had already been to the ranch and arrested five of the ranch hands including the manager--all of them charged in an elaborate operation of trafficking illegals out of Mexico and to points north.

Her former in-laws looked sick. Carolann was a little too ashen as tears ran down her face. Abby feared she was having chest pain and was hiding it. She'd catch her wincing every now and again. Frank's health wasn't much better. His Parkinson's was taking its toll in his agitated state. Usually, the shaking was under control, but tonight he shook like a drunk coming off a bad binge.

In the thirty years she could remember the man being in her life, she'd never seen him cry. Until now.

Their son had disgraced them beyond belief. And the man who had become an adopted member of the family had been rushed to surgery. Put there by their son.

Despite the early morning hour, the waiting room was packed. Two TVs bolted to the walls played and replayed the news coverage of the hell she and her family had survived only four hours ago. Not only had they made the local news, CNN and FOX had the shooting of country star Seth Kendall by the McAllister County Sheriff as breaking news.

She turned away from the scenes as a doctor entered the room. She untangled Emily's arms from around her and stood. "Dr. Weber?"

The surgeon smiled and took her hand. "Abby, it's been a long time."

She and Bruce Weber had worked together years ago. "How is he?"

Emily stood beside her and wrapped her arms around her. "Is my--my dad gonna be okay?"

Bruce puckered his brow as if in confusion but turned on a charming smile and nodded. "Mr. Knight will be fine," he said, referring to the name under which Seth was registered for privacy purposes. The bullet had gone straight through, but Seth had lost a lot of blood and had been rushed to surgery to close the wound. "The surgery went smoothly, and I don't foresee any lasting damage."

"Thank God!" Carolann put her hand over her heart.

Abby closed her eyes and prayed a silent thank you.

"Can we see him?" Emily asked.

Bruce smiled and nodded. "Yes, he's been asking about you."

Abby and Emily entered the private room. Seth lay in a bed with his right arm in a sling. An IV dripped into the back of his left hand, and he looked silly in the bright teal hospital gown, but Abby had never been so glad to see him.

Emily rushed ahead and came up short at the bed. He reached out with his left hand, and she took it. "I was so afraid."

He smiled and brought her fingers to his lips. "Me, too, sunshine. I didn't want him to hurt you."

She sat on the edge of the bed and touched his face. "How could he--he want to sell me?"

He pulled her down to his chest and caressed her hair. "I don't know, honey. But you aren't going anywhere."

"You saved me." Emily lifted her head and looked into his face.

"I'm your father. I'd gladly die for you."

Emily sniffed and big tears rolled down her face. "I love you."

Sara Walter Ellwood

Seth made a choking sound and pulled her to him again. "I love you too."

He looked up at Abby as she wiped away the tears in her eyes. She took his hand and touched Emily's shoulder. "I love you both."

Emily moved and Abby sat beside him.

He got his emotions under control and smiled as he looked from Emily to Abby. "Don't you think it's about time the three of us become a family?"

Careful not to put too much pressure on the IV in the back of his hand, she gently squeezed. "We already are."

"I was thinking something permanent and legal."

Her heart skipped a beat. "What do you have in mind?"

"Emily, can you find my jeans? They should be in the drawer over there."

Emily did as asked and then peered over her shoulder at him.

"In the right front pocket you'll find something. Get it and bring it here."

Emily muttered, "Holy crap."

Abby couldn't pull her gaze from his to see what excited Emily. He let go of her hand and Emily dropped a ring into his palm.

As he held the diamond ring out to her, Abby gasped. "I'll probably wish I'd waited to do this and been a little more romantic about it, but I can't wait any longer. I don't want to live without you." He glanced at Emily, who was behind her. "Either one of you. I've been doing that for far too long already."

Her heart jumped into her throat, and she covered her mouth with her hand to keep it from escaping.

"Abigail, will you marry me?"

She lost her breath and could do nothing but nod. She held out her shaking left hand and he slipped the ring onto her finger.

He smiled. "I'll take that as a yes."

Emily whooped and kissed first her and then Seth on their cheeks. "Of course it's a yes!"

Abby giggled and stared down into the beautiful eyes of the man she loved while time seemed to slow.

"Well, aren't you gonna kiss him, Momma?"

He grinned and slipped his arm around her waist. "Yeah, aren't you gonna kiss me?"

"For the rest of my life." She leaned forward and brushed her lips against his.

He held her against him and kissed her with a restrained passion that promised so much more.

He broke the kiss, and she lifted her hand to get a better look at the huge marquis cut diamond with round diamonds on either side of it. "Sweet mercy, this thing's a rock! Seth, I can't wear this. I'll lose it. Or be mugged. Dear Lord!"

"You won't get mugged, and it's insured in case you misplace it." He laughed and brushed his fingers over her face. "I guess it's a little ostentatious, but I wanted it to be a symbol of how much I love you. I actually thought it was small when I compared it to how I feel about you."

She drew her gaze from the brilliant ring to look into his vibrant eyes. "I don't need a diamond the size of Texas to know how much you love me, Seth. I can see it in your eyes and feel it in your touch. I hope you'll never doubt my love for you." She couldn't keep the tears from falling as she reached for a sobbing Emily and pulled her close. "We're finally a family and that's all that matters."

Sara Walter Ellwood

Although Sara Walter Ellwood has long ago left the farm for the glamour of the big town, she draws on her experiences growing up on a small hobby farm in West Central Pennsylvania to write her stories. She's been married to her college sweetheart for nearly 20 years, and they have two teenagers and one very spoiled rescue cat named Penny. She longs to visit the places she writes about and jokes she's a cowgirl at heart stuck in Pennsylvania suburbia.

She also writes paranormal romantic suspense under the pen name of Cera duBois.